MW00809417

Where I Belong

Copyright © 2018 by Mirror Press, LLC

Print Edition

All rights reserved

No part of this book may be reproduced in any form whatsoever without prior written permission of the publisher, except in the case of brief passages embodied in critical reviews and articles. This is a work of fiction. The characters, names, incidents, places, and dialogue are products of the author's imagination and are not to be construed as real.

Interior design by Cora Johnson

Edited by Cassidy Wadsworth Skousen and Lisa Shepherd

Cover design by Rachael Anderson

Cover image credit: Deposit Photos #62592897

Published by Mirror Press, LLC

ISBN-13: 978-1-947152-28-1

Where I Belong

A PINE VALLEY NOVEL

Heather B. Moore

Mirror Press

PINE VALLEY SERIES

Worth the Risk

Where I Belong

Say You Love Me

Where I Belong

Jane Morris makes a living by cleaning the houses of the wealthy residents of Pine Valley, and she tries hard not to judge their extravagant lifestyles. But when one of her clients goes through a devastating breakup with his fiancée, Jane finds herself in the middle of his emotional mess. She wants to help him, but Cameron Vance is a man she could easily lose her heart to. Jane agrees to be his date to the charity event of the year, organized by Cameron's mother. But the magical night shows Jane that if she's a Cinderella, then Cameron is definitely a candidate for Prince Charming.

One

"Wow, this is the set-up."
    "Are you kidding me, man?"
"You're a lucky guy."
"It's about time."
"She looks expensive."
"I can't believe you're actually getting married."
"Didn't you just meet a couple of months ago?"
"Congratulations, my friend."

Cameron Vance's head hurt, but he smiled through the comments—the same comments over and over. He smiled, he laughed, he slapped backs, he accepted congratulations, he joked, and he held Crystal's hand as they answered question after question. Granted, his answers were much less enthusiastic than hers. He didn't necessarily like huge crowds at his newly renovated cabin in Pine Valley. But Crystal had insisted.

Engagement parties were wedding protocol, and she was all about protocol.

"Oh, there's the guy that sold your condo," Crystal cooed in Cameron's ear. There were at least fifty people on the main floor of the cabin, and that plus the blaring music made it hard to carry a conversation.

Cameron turned to look toward the front door. Jeff Finch, the real estate agent, had arrived, and as he approached, one of Crystal's friends drew her away to talk about the upcoming honeymoon to Vail, Colorado.

"Jeff, welcome," Cameron said, shaking the man's hand.

Jeff's blue eyes focused on Cameron, and he smiled. "Congratulations. I didn't even know you had a serious girlfriend when I last talked to you. The renovation is incredible, by the way."

Cameron chuckled. It was August now, and he'd had a whole construction crew working around the clock so that he wouldn't have to move twice when he got married. "Thanks for hooking me up with Grant Shelton," he said. "He and his brother-in-law do great work."

Jeff nodded. "I'm glad." His gaze shifted to Crystal.

Cameron looked her way too. Even if no one knew her, it was obvious Crystal was the bride-to-be, since she took every chance she got to show off her three-carat diamond ring.

"Is that the lucky lady?" Jeff asked.

"Yeah, that's Crystal," Cameron said, seeing her as Jeff must see her. Blonde, blue-eyed, petite, and energetic. She talked a mile a minute when she was excited, and her favorite thing to do was make plans. Plans for the wedding, plans for the honeymoon, plans for their future.

"Is she from Pine Valley?"

"No," Cameron said. "We met at a friend's party a couple of months back." He didn't miss the surprise on Jeff's face.

"A *couple of months*? And you're getting married in *September*?"

Cameron swallowed. It had all gone so fast—a whirlwind, really. His mom had commented that Crystal must have had her dress and ring picked out the first week they started dating. And that was saying a lot from his mom, since she was the most organized and efficient woman he knew.

But Cameron had been quick to defend Crystal. When they met, she hadn't known that he was from a wealthy family and ran two of his dad's clothing manufacturing companies. She wasn't a fortune hunter or anything. She had her own money.

"When it's right, it's right," Cameron told Jeff with a laugh.

Jeff didn't look convinced, but he smiled. "Well, congratulations. I hope the two of you will be happy."

"Thanks," Cameron said. "The bar is over there—feel free to get what you want and mingle. Lots of single ladies here tonight."

Jeff nodded. "I've got some timeshare hookups if you're looking for a place for a honeymoon, but you probably have it all worked out."

"Oh yeah, we do," Cameron said. "My dad has a place in Vail, Colorado. Crystal wasn't too excited at first, since it's a mountain resort town like Pine Valley. But she'll love it."

"I'll love what?" Crystal said, coming up to Cameron and looking with bright interest at Jeff Finch. She looped her arm through Cameron's and settled in close to him. "You're the realtor, right?"

"That's me," Jeff said.

Crystal's laugh tinkled as she extended her hand to shake Jeff's. "I've seen your pictures and signs all over."

Jeff shook her hand. "Nice to meet you."

"I'm so glad you could come to our party," Crystal said.

"Sorry the place is so cramped. Cameron and I have talked about adding a couple of extra rooms."

Crystal had talked about it, but Cameron didn't see the need. He was ready to move on from the renovation and not start up any new project for a while. It had already taken time enough away from his work schedule.

Jeff looked surprised at Crystal's comment. "I think the place is great as is. It's really beautiful."

Cameron agreed.

"It *is* great." Crystal wrinkled her nose. "Too small, though."

Jeff opened his mouth, then shut it. He looked at Cameron, an eyebrow lifted.

What? Cameron wanted to say. But his head hurt, and he didn't want to get into a tiff with Crystal at their engagement party. Besides, his parents had just arrived.

"Well, congratulations again, you two," Jeff said. "I'll be out of town during your wedding, but if I don't see you before then, I hope you enjoy Vail. I hear it's beautiful in September."

"Thanks, we will. And thanks for coming tonight," Cameron said.

Jeff moved away, mixing into the crowd.

Cameron's parents were making their way toward them but were stalled by a mutual friend who greeted them. Cameron was impressed his father had come tonight. Cameron had told him this party wasn't a must-attend—it had been a last-minute thing Crystal had suddenly planned. So it was sweet of his parents to make the effort.

"Honey?" Crystal said next to him.

He looked down at her.

"You need to stop telling people about Vail," she said. "I mean, we haven't completely decided."

Cameron blinked. "What do you mean, we haven't

decided? The place is booked, and we were just talking about it yesterday."

Crystal smiled that smile of hers that meant she was trying to be sweet although she completely disagreed. "Remember how I told you my friend Deeann went to Italy on her honeymoon last spring? She said it was absolutely amazing. They spent ten days—"

"Crystal," Cameron cut her off. "You know I can't be gone for ten days—especially in another time zone and across the ocean."

"Cameron, this place looks beautiful!" a woman's voice cut in. "I love what you've done with it."

Cameron turned to see his mom. They shared the same brown eyes and dark brown hair. "Thanks, Mom," he said. "Hi, Dad."

His dad grinned and pulled him into a bear hug. "You've been busy, I see. Even Grandpa Vance would be impressed with what you've done to his old cabin. Good thing the quarterly numbers showed a profit, or we'd be having a serious discussion right now."

Cameron pulled away from his dad and laughed. "I told you it was going to be a good quarter. The Adidas contract we signed in March is only the beginning of more great things to come. I have a meeting with Under Armour next week to see if they're interested in contracting with us for manufacturing as well."

"That's my boy," his dad said in a jovial tone, clapping Cameron on the shoulder.

"Excuse me, Mr. Vance," Crystal said. "I don't mean to be rude, but tonight Cameron promised *not* to talk about business. We're focusing on celebrating our engagement."

Cameron vaguely remembered agreeing to something, but the silence that fell within their small circle was palpable.

"All righty, then," his dad said, his mouth still smiling, but his eyes gleaming with several questions Cameron knew he wasn't looking forward to answering later.

"We'll go hit the refreshments since we had to leave another dinner party early to come here," his mom said, ever the tactful person. "Crystal, dear, did you put the refreshments together? They look wonderful."

Crystal straightened but still clung to Cameron's arm. "I used a catering company."

"Of course you did," his mom said with a sweet smile. "But it still takes time and effort to put everything together. It all looks very nice."

"Thank you, Mrs. Vance."

Even though Crystal's tone was pleasant, Cameron felt her stiffen at his side. He didn't know why Crystal felt defensive around his mom. As far as he was concerned, his mom was a genuine and capable person. She sat on several boards of companies his dad owned under his parent company Vance Enterprises. She also ran the charity division of VE and was always bringing people and opportunities together.

As his parents moved away, Cameron suddenly felt stifled in this crowded room. He just wanted to go out onto the back deck and breathe in nature. He'd had several alterations made to the backyard as well, adding a fountain and a stepped terrace. A couple of fire pits were strategically placed, affording a great area for get-togethers.

He knew there were a couple of dozen people out there, but it was way less crowded than inside the cabin. "Let's go outside for a little bit," Cameron said to Crystal.

Her lips pursed into a pout that Cameron knew well. He remembered her Italy comment and wanted to groan. He didn't want to discuss this here and now. Anger shot through him, and he determined not to give into this point of debate. He'd already given in to plenty.

"I should talk to Dawson, and I think he went outside," Cameron continued, tamping down his frustrations. "I told him I'd introduce him to my dad."

"That lawyer guy?" Crystal's expression went into a full pout. "He's so full of himself."

Cameron felt like he'd been slapped. He and Dawson weren't best friends or anything, but his dad needed some legal counsel on one of his employees who'd been caught stealing last week at one of the manufacturing plants. Cameron leaned down and kissed Crystal on the cheek. "I'll be back in a little bit then," he said firmly and walked away.

His mind spun with a dozen thoughts as he moved toward the back doors, greeting friends as he went.

Someone bumped into him and dropped whatever she was carrying. "Oh, sorry," a woman said, bending to pick up a plastic bag that looked like it was full of dirty napkins and empty plastic cups.

Cameron recognized her as the woman Crystal had hired to clean the cabin once a week. Her name was Jennie or Jackie, or something.

Her dark green eyes widened as she looked at him. "Oh, Mr. Vance. I didn't mean to bump into you."

She was probably about twenty-five or twenty-six, only a few years younger than he, yet she was always so formal around him.

"No, it's my fault . . ." He glanced at the trash bag she was carrying. And then he noticed her name tag: *Jane.* "Crystal hired you for tonight?"

"Yes." She reached up to smooth back her nearly black hair. Jane was pretty in a natural way. Her eyes were framed by thick eyelashes, and she didn't wear a bit of makeup. Yet her cheeks had a natural pink to them, and her full lips . . . well, he shouldn't be paying such close attention.

Cameron blinked and cleared his thoughts. "Oh, I didn't realize. Well, thank you. I appreciate your help."

Tiny lines appeared between her brows. "You do know I'm getting paid to work here, don't you, Mr. Vance?"

"Yeah, of course," Cameron said. "It's okay to thank people who are working for me—especially ones who have to clean up after my mess."

The lines between her brows disappeared, and she smiled. "Then you're very welcome, sir."

"Jane," he said, touching her arm. "That's your name, right?"

She nodded, and he couldn't help but notice the faint blush on her cheeks.

"Please call me Cameron. Mr. Vance is my dad."

"Oh, okay." Her mouth rounded in an O.

Cameron suddenly knew that any makeup on this woman would only detract from her natural beauty. Her plain white blouse and black pants might make another woman fade into the background, but not Jane.

"I'll try to remember that, sir. I mean, Cameron." She gave him an apologetic smile; then her gaze shifted. "I should get back to work. Thank you."

He was about to ask her what she was thanking *him* for when he saw Crystal hurrying toward him, a broad smile on her face.

"You won't believe who I just talked to," she said, grasping his hand. "My friend Lacey is a travel agent, and she told me that there's a fantastic package to Italy in September. Come on, you've got to meet her and hear what she says."

As Crystal tugged him through the gathering to the other side of the room, Cameron wondered how long it would take for the place to clear out if he accidentally set off a smoke detector.

Two

"Come back in the morning," Crystal had told Jane the night before. "My fiancé and I want some privacy. Although frankly, I thought this place would be cleaned up by now . . ."

Those words still rang in Jane's mind the next morning as she pulled up to the Vance cabin near the exclusive Pine Valley Ski Resort. She climbed out of her car that had seen better days, but since she didn't drive long distances, the car was fine. And she liked the maid service logo painted on the side: *The Cleaning Lady*, along with her website. She grabbed the utility bag that sported the same logo out of the back seat.

Jane knew it was a generic name, but it left no doubt what type of business she ran. She stood for a moment and looked up at the sprawling cabin before her. Crystal had told Jane that the cabin had been in the Vance family for decades, and it had been a dinky little thing until Cameron had done a massive renovation. Now it was more of a mini-mansion cabin, which was the case for this side of the mountain. And Cameron Vance was just another wealthy person who Jane cleaned for, although technically his fiancée had hired her.

Jane was by no means complaining. She loved the flexibility of her job and the ability it gave her to help her dad financially. His retirement got him by, but with his advanced diabetes, he had extra expenses and had a hard time getting around now with the pain in his legs. She wished more than once that she'd moved to Pine Valley sooner. But this had been her dad's home with his new wife for the past eleven years, and it was always a sore point when Jane came to visit her dad.

Her parents had divorced when she was fifteen, and her dad had remarried soon after, leaving her mom devastated. When Jane had attended her stepmom's funeral two years before, Jane was shocked at her dad's decline in health. She had to practically force him to retire from his assistant manager position at a discount store. Being on his feet most of the day wasn't keeping him healthy.

At first, she'd worked at the resort hotel as a maid, and one thing led to another as she took on a couple of private clients. Now she had her own maid service, and only herself as an employee, but Jane wouldn't have it any other way. She could make sure that her dad ate nutritious meals and exercised twice a day, and in general her company staved off his gloomy moods. In turn, she was developing a relationship with him that she'd never had as a child, when it seemed all her parents did was fight.

Jane made her way to the cabin's front porch and walked up the pine steps. The remodel was beautiful, and Jane enjoyed working and cleaning in such a beautiful home. She just felt a little sorry for Cameron Vance. Irony at its best, she decided. Why should she feel sorry for a fabulously wealthy, gorgeous man who was in the prime of his life? His parents seemed equally incredible.

And Jane could have easily finished cleaning up in about forty-five minutes last night if Crystal hadn't kicked her out. Jane sighed and knocked on the front door, hoping that 8:30 a.m. wasn't too early. But she had a full day of clients ahead of her, and this was the only time she could squeeze in the Vance cabin.

No one answered the door after her first knock. Crystal's Mercedes wasn't in its usual spot in the driveway, so she must have gone home last night. Jane wondered if she should just text Crystal that she'd stopped by, but then the door cracked open.

"Yes?" a scratchy male voice said. Then the door opened wider. "Oh, hi."

It was obvious that Cameron Vance had just woken up. First, he wore only a pair of pajama bottoms. Jane refused to ogle his sculpted chest, refocusing on his face. He towered over her, his brown hair a messy mop that was sort of boyish and made him look younger. His light brown eyes were probably what Jane liked best about the man—if she was going to admit to liking anything about him. They were so expressive, clear, and strangely trustworthy. And that was saying something when he existed in the world of the social elite.

Jane had quit on clients who creeped her out just by the way they looked at her.

"I hope I didn't wake you," Jane rushed to say as she cringed inside. "I'm here to finish cleaning up from last night."

"Did Crystal tell you to come back?" Cameron said.

"Yes, she told me to come this morning, but I can return

later," Jane said. "It probably won't be until about 4:30 though."

"No," Cameron said. "You can come in now. I just didn't know you were coming." He opened the door wider, waiting for her to enter.

She hesitated.

"Come on," he said, his voice sounding more normal and less hoarse now. "I haven't had my coffee, but I won't bite."

Jane squared her shoulders and stepped past him, noticing how he still had a clean spice scent even though he likely hadn't showered this morning. She liked a clean-smelling man. But that was neither here nor there. Not only was Cameron Vance way out of her league, he was marrying a trophy wife.

She walked through the living room to the kitchen, where she set her utility bag on the granite countertop. Then she did a slow spin and looked around. It was a lot cleaner than she'd left it. The empty containers and dirty cups and plates were all gone. The counters had been wiped off, and all Jane could see that needed to be done in the kitchen was sweeping and washing some serving utensils soaking in the sink.

Then the flashing lights on the dishwasher caught her eye—a cycle had already completed. She turned to see Cameron walking into the kitchen. He crossed to the far counter and turned on the coffee maker. He was still shirtless, and Jane couldn't help but watch him reach for a coffee cup from the cupboard. He must lift weights, or run, or run and lift weights.

She swallowed. "Did you guys clean up last night? I didn't do all of this."

Cameron turned, coffee cup in hand. "I couldn't sleep after . . . Well, I cleaned up the trash and loaded the dishwasher." His mouth quirked into a half-smile, which sent a knot of fire through Jane's stomach. "I *can* clean, you know. I've been taking out trash since I was about five years old."

"I've no doubt that you can clean," Jane said, then wanted to smack herself. What was she saying? She moved to the kitchen pantry, where the broom was stored. "I'll just get started so I can get out of your way." As her back was turned to Cameron, she heard the scrape of one of the barstools at the island. Was he going to *sit down*?

She grabbed the broom and turned. Yep. He was sitting at the island, running a hand through his hair. Was he going to just sit there and watch her clean? Would it be rude to ask him to put on a shirt?

She gripped the broom a little tighter than necessary as she started to sweep the room from the edges to the center by the stove. Yep. Cameron Vance was still sitting there, seeming lost in his thoughts.

He looked tired, she decided, more tired than he should after a great engagement party and probably an equally great late night with Crystal. He looked weary.

Jane knew it was none of her business, but she asked, "Are you all right, Mr. Vance?"

His head lifted, and he looked over at her.

Jane wondered how a man could still look so great with no grooming or shower. But his eyes were not quite right.

"Actually, I'm kind of a mess." He gave a half-laugh that wasn't humorous at all. "Crystal and I got into a pretty major fight last night. Turns out she booked our honeymoon to Italy behind my back."

Jane didn't reply. She hadn't expected such a confession from a man she hardly knew. And she didn't know what was good or bad in the world of the wealthy. A honeymoon to Italy sounded pretty extravagant, but maybe Crystal meant it as one of those huge surprises?

"I told her I could only take a four- or five-day honeymoon. September is end of quarter. She agreed to go to Vail. At least, I thought she did." He rubbed a hand over his face. "Sorry. I'm rambling, and you probably don't want to hear about my drama so early in the morning. I don't even want to think about it myself."

The coffeemaker timer went off.

"I'll get that," Jane said, moving toward the counter. She picked up his coffee mug and filled it, then set it in front of him.

"Thanks," he said, staring down into the mug.

"Do you want anything added to it?" Jane asked, wishing she'd thought of it sooner.

"No, black is fine. Perfect for today, actually." He took a sip, then grimaced. "Have you ever felt like your life is spinning out of control?"

Jane heard him but didn't exactly know if he was talking to her. He spoke quietly, not looking at her. But her sympathy went out to him. No matter what she'd thought of him for being wealthy, she could see that he was discouraged right now.

She leaned against the counter. Then after a moment she said, "When I was fifteen and my parents divorced, I felt like the ground had swallowed me up. I was suddenly living in a tiny apartment with a very angry mother, and nothing I said or did was right. My parents made every decision for me and used me as a pawn in their bitterness." She exhaled. She hadn't meant to dump quite so much out there. But Cameron was studying her with interest. "I know it's not the same thing," she continued, "but I can maybe relate a little bit to feeling like things are moving faster than you want them to."

Cameron nodded. "That's exactly how I feel. Everything feels rushed—work, family, Crystal . . . I'm constantly trying to juggle a dozen different things at a time. The only reason I'm sitting here, wallowing in my coffee, is because you knocked on the door. My phone is upstairs, probably buzzing with a hundred emails and texts."

Jane straightened. "Can you push the wedding back?"

"Ha. Ha." Cameron deadpanned. "If only things were that simple." He went back to staring into space again.

Jane moved quietly back to where she'd left the broom. She started sweeping again, and by the time she reached the kitchen table, Cameron stood and came over to pull out the chairs.

"You don't have to do that," she said.

He shrugged. "I've always had a hard time watching someone cleaning up while I'm just sitting around."

"Sitting around, avoiding your hundreds of emails and texts?"

His brown eyes crinkled at the corners, and he almost smiled. "Exactly."

When Jane finished sweeping, she vacuumed the great room. Cameron was nowhere in sight when she was done. Even his coffee cup was rinsed out and sitting in the sink. She did a quick check of the backyard but only had to straighten some of the chairs. There was no garbage in sight. She took a moment to look at the beautiful pine trees climbing the hill behind the house. This cabin was really secluded, yet it felt like an estate at the same time.

She walked into the main house again just as Cameron was coming down the stairs.

His hair was damp, and he was wearing jeans and a faded-blue T-shirt. He'd obviously showered.

"I'll get the door," he said.

Jane hadn't even heard it. She was finished working, though, and she went into the kitchen to grab her utility bag.

"Sweetheart," she heard a woman say from the front room. *Crystal's voice.*

Jane froze where she was, not wanting to interrupt their conversation by coming out of the kitchen.

"I tried to get here early before you had breakfast," Crystal said. "Why aren't you dressed?"

"What's going on?" Cameron said, his tone sounding defensive.

"I brought you breakfast," Crystal said, then suddenly she was walking into the kitchen. "I knew you'd be grumpy." She stopped cold when she saw Jane, and Crystal's smile dropped. "What are you doing here?"

"She's cleaning up like you asked her to," Cameron said, walking in behind Crystal, his arms folded. And he didn't look happy.

Crystal's eyes narrowed. "Oh, that's right. You can go home now."

Jane gave her best fake smile. "I was just leaving."

She moved past Cameron, glad that she didn't have to remain in Crystal's presence any longer. As Jane walked to the front door, she felt Cameron's gaze on her, but there was nothing she could do. Cameron had to work things out with Crystal on his own.

As Jane climbed into her car, she had to laugh at the crazy couple inside that beautiful cabin. Apparently having money brought nothing close to happiness.

Three

Cameron had the strangest urge to ditch Crystal in his kitchen and catch a ride with Jane. He'd go wherever she was going. He just didn't want to be where he was.

"So, I brought all your favorites—but you have to guess the theme," Crystal said.

Cameron watched her pull out plastic containers from the large sack she carried.

"Sausage omelets, sourdough baguettes, soft cheese, spicy hot chocolate . . . do you get it?"

Cameron said nothing.

"It's an Italian breakfast!" Crystal crossed to him and looped her arms about his neck. "Let's kiss and make up. I talked to Lacey. She said that we could do a six-day honeymoon, and she'll book us into hotels that have modern things like Wi-Fi." She raised up on her toes so that she was eye to eye with Cameron. "Then you can work your little hiney off on our honeymoon while I'm gazing at the David statue."

Cameron wrapped his hands around Crystal's wrists and moved her arms down. She drew away, her brows furrowing as she went into full pout mode.

"Six days means eight days because of travel," he said. "It also means I'll be working when you're sleeping."

Crystal shrugged. "I'm sure it will all work out. Let's just get there and play it by ear."

He exhaled. "I don't play my career by ear. I wouldn't be living in this type of place if I did."

"Just think of the food," Crystal pressed. "I mean, it would be ten times better than this."

She pointed to the food on the counter that was, frankly, churning Cameron's stomach. Maybe he was coming down with something, but coffee was all that he could manage this morning.

Crystal was watching him closely, as if trying to determine how much she could push him. It frustrated him that she'd ignored his wishes and then gone behind his back to meet with a travel agent.

"Look, honey," she said, moving close again. "Worst case, if you have to get back, we'll change our flights and come home early." She pressed herself against him and whispered in his ear, "We can always have a second honeymoon later."

Cameron was tired. His headache was back. He needed more sleep. And maybe he should eat something. He also couldn't believe he was about to give in to Crystal on this. "All right," he said. "Tell the travel agent five days, four nights, and not a minute longer."

Crystal squealed and threw her arms about him. She kissed him on the mouth, and Cameron wondered why, when he should have been feeling joy at planning a honeymoon in one of the most romantic places in the world, all he felt was frustration.

Crystal didn't leave for another hour, and when she did, Cameron sat at the kitchen counter with his laptop while he worked through replying to about fifty emails. Not quite the hundreds he'd told Jane about. He smiled to himself when he thought about their conversation. If there was ever a woman more different than Crystal, it was Jane.

Life was interesting, he decided. One person's life experiences could change a person. He thought of Jane being a pawn between her divorced parents. He supposed a lot of kids went through that sort of thing. He knew Crystal's parents were divorced too, but she had never really brought up the topic. Whenever they were together, Crystal was focused on herself and Cameron. It was like she was building her own little kingdom. Cameron just didn't know who the king was.

When Crystal called a few hours later, he listened with half an ear as she rattled off the itinerary the travel agent had put together.

"So, I have a bunch of brochures for all the places I want to visit. I'll be there around 5:00 to show you," she said. "Should I bring Chinese?"

Cameron realized he hadn't been paying attention the last few moments. "Wait. What?"

"It's our date night, silly, but I know that you're buried with work, so I'm bringing dinner to you."

"I don't think—"

"You need to eat, and I *am* your fiancée," Crystal said. "I'll even let you decide how long or how short our date is, but you might want to see what I'm wearing first."

He glanced at the clock over the kitchen stove. He knew once she came over, it would be hard to get rid of her. "7:00 would work better."

Crystal laughed—what did that mean? "All right, sweetie.

See you soon. And just so you know, the maid will be coming in the morning to wash all the new bedding in the cabin."

"Do you mean Jane?"

"Yes, that's her," she said. "New bedding should be cleaned before it's used."

She hung up before Cameron could ask her to clarify. He didn't know why he was so edgy. He'd agreed to Italy, but it was the whole decision-making process that bothered him. He closed his eyes and exhaled. Then he found himself thinking through his entire relationship with Crystal.

They'd met at a charity event, and Crystal had been sweet and flirtatious, not to mention gorgeous. They'd both bid on the same golf package and gotten into a small bidding war. Cameron had finally conceded and let her win the package. After the auction was over, Crystal had come up to him and invited him to meet her on the golf course so they could share the package.

Cameron had found that brilliant, and their flirting had continued throughout the night. Less than a week later, they had their golf date, and things had escalated from there. Crystal had quickly inserted herself into every aspect of his life, while Cameron was swamped with the cabin renovations and work with the manufacturing plants. She'd attended a company dinner with him, and suddenly, they were a couple.

And now, they were getting married in less than a month.

Cameron shook his head. He was thirty and had never really pursued marriage, since he was so focused on building his career and showing his dad that he was up to the task of running the plants.

His phone rang. It was his mom, but just then someone knocked on the door. Cameron left the phone on the counter while he went to answer the door. He'd call her back later. Cameron opened the front door to see a man in a delivery service uniform standing there, with an embroidered name badge saying *Robert*. Had Crystal ordered the food already? But the man wasn't carrying any food.

"Are you Cameron Vance?" the man named Robert asked, looking down at a clipboard he held.

"Yes, that's me."

"I have a delivery for you," Robert said. "Can you sign the invoice, then I'll guide the truck up here? I didn't want to back it into your driveway until I knew this was the right residence."

Cameron took the clipboard from Robert and looked down at the itemized invoice. It was a list of furniture . . . couches, tables, lamps, an area rug, bar stools, two armoires . . . "I'm afraid you have the wrong place. I didn't order any of this furniture." He flipped to the second page. More furniture pieces were listed, and then the total of $35,000. His eyes about popped out. Someone was furnishing their entire home. He flipped back to the first page and looked at the top. Sure enough, it was his name and address at the top of the invoice. "Uh, I still didn't order this." He looked up at the delivery man. "Who came into your store?"

Robert shrugged. "I'm not a sales person, just the delivery service. Maybe it was your, uh, wife?" He looked past Cameron, as if there might be a wife standing behind him.

"I'm not married," Cameron said. "Can you call the store to find out? I'd like to know how this invoice has my name and address on it, and how this was all paid for."

"Sure thing," Robert said, pulling a phone out of his pocket. As he made the call, a truck that was the size of a moving truck came up the road. It stopped in front of Cameron's place and started to reverse into the driveway. "Wait," Cameron said, moving past the man on his porch and trying to catch the truck driver's attention. He hurried to the passenger's side of the truck, where another man was peering out at him. Cameron knocked on the window. "This isn't my delivery," he called up.

The driver braked, and both men rolled down their windows. "This isn't my delivery. The other guy is calling the store to find out what's going on.'"

"Mr. Vance?" someone said behind him.

Cameron turned to see Robert.

"It appears that there's been a mix-up."

Cameron exhaled with relief. "Yes, that's what I thought. What happened?"

"Your *wife,* Crystal Vance, ordered the furniture a couple of days ago," Robert said, giving him a stern look. "We were supposed to deliver it in two weeks, so it's with my apologies that we're so early and caught you unawares."

Cameron's mouth fell open.

"If it's not too much of a bother, we'd like to complete this delivery today, since we already have it loaded in the truck," Robert continued. "We could store it in your garage if your house isn't ready. Then we could come back later and move it inside. That would be an extra charge though."

Cameron swallowed. "How was the invoice charged?"

Robert looked down at the invoice. "It says here that there was a $5,000 down payment charged to your American Express, and the rest of the payment will go through upon receipt of the merchandise."

"She has my credit card?" Cameron felt his pockets. His wallet was in the house. "Hang on." He sprinted back to the cabin and pounded up the stairs to the second level. In his bedroom, he located his wallet and opened it. His American Express card was gone.

Cameron sank onto his bed as numbness settled over him. Apparently Crystal had taken his credit card and gone shopping to replace all of the furniture in his cabin. The furniture was to be delivered in two weeks . . . When was she going to tell him?

Heat spread through his face and neck. She'd taken his credit card without asking. She might be his fiancée, but they weren't married yet. Technically, this was stealing. And even if they *had* been married, weren't things like replacing an entire cabin full of furniture something they should discuss in advance?

He closed his eyes and tried to calm his erratic breathing and racing heart. He'd never been so angry in his life. First, he had to get rid of the moving truck. Standing from his bed, he steeled his emotions and walked back down the stairs. Outside, the three men were standing at the rear of the truck. They'd opened the truck's hatch, and Cameron caught a view of an entire load of furniture.

"There's been a huge misunderstanding," Cameron said in a clipped voice. "I will pay the delivery charge, but you need to return the furniture. It's been ordered by mistake."

Robert stared at Cameron as if he was speaking a different language. "Sir, we'd be happy to unload everything to your garage. It's no trouble."

"Call your manager back, please," Cameron said. "I'll explain what's happened."

Robert handed over his phone, and when the manager answered, Cameron used all his self-control to explain that the woman who made the purchase was *not* his wife and, more significantly, her name was not on his credit card.

The manager apologized profusely, but Cameron wasn't interested in apologies from the wrong person.

"Sorry about all of this," he said to Robert when he was off the phone. "You went through a lot of trouble, but I'm glad I caught it now."

Robert instructed his men to close the hatch, and a few minutes later Cameron watched the truck disappear down the road.

He walked slowly back to the cabin. Without going inside, he shut the door and walked around to the backyard. He climbed the steps of the deck, then sat on the top step. The shade from the overhead awning kept the summer heat off Cameron, but he was still burning up inside. He scrubbed his hands through his hair, then propped his elbows on his knees.

This had all been a mistake. *Crystal* was a mistake. Taking his credit card and buying $35,000 worth of furniture wasn't even the whole reason that he knew he could no longer marry her. She'd thought she could replace something he loved without even asking him. Did she even care that although the furniture in the cabin might be older, it was sentimental? This cabin had been his grandparents'. He had many fond memories of the original place. He had expanded it, upgraded it, but the furniture stayed. He wasn't going to budge on that.

It was time to call Crystal.

Four

No one answered the door at Jane's first knock. This time, it was 11:00 in the morning, and Cameron should be awake. Unless he wasn't here. But with the garage doors closed, Jane had no way of knowing if he was home. Crystal's car wasn't in sight either.

Jane looked at her phone to check her text messages again. Sure enough, there was Crystal's request for all the bedding to be laundered at the cabin this morning. Jane had taken care of another client's house this morning so that she didn't run the risk of waking up Cameron Vance again. Maybe she was too late instead.

Jane knocked a second time, but still no answer. She stepped off the porch and made her way back to the car. She'd text Crystal and wait a few minutes to see if she replied. But before she did, she thought she heard the echo of music playing. Jane stopped and listened. Yep. Music was playing— from the backyard?

She walked around the cabin, picking her way along a narrow gravel path lined with various bushes. As she neared the yard, the music grew louder. She rounded the corner of the cabin, and at first she didn't see anyone. Then she noticed a form on the hammock that stretched between two of the trees. Next to the hammock was a litter of beer bottles and what looked like Chinese take-out containers.

Jane took a couple of steps forward to see that Cameron was sound asleep in the hammock. She paused. He looked exhausted, even in his sleep. His phone was next to him, playing music, and obviously he'd fallen asleep to it.

She was about to turn away and leave him in peace when he opened his eyes. He blinked a couple of times.

"Sorry, I didn't mean to wake you," Jane said, taking another step back. "No one answered the door when I knocked, and I heard the music coming from the backyard, so I came to see if anyone was home."

Cameron just stared at her for a moment. His eyes were rimmed red, and there were dark circles beneath them.

"I can talk to Crystal about a better time to wash the bedding," she said.

"No," he said in a gruff voice. Then he cleared his throat. "You can do the bedding now." He moved to a sitting position.

His hair was wild from sleeping on the hammock, and Jane would have laughed if he didn't look so distressed.

"I didn't mean to fall asleep out here," he said, his voice still raspy. He scrubbed a hand through his hair. "One thing led to another, I guess."

Jane followed his gaze to the deck. Her eyes widened at the sight of broken glass scattered across it. She quickly looked back at him, scanning for any injuries. "Are you all right?"

His brown eyes met hers. "Funny you should ask that."

She waited, her breathing feeling shallow. Had he gotten drunk and smashed things?

"Crystal and I broke up last night. She might have thrown a few things at me." He rubbed at his face and groaned. "I think I have a migraine."

Jane stared at him. She wanted to ask him what happened. She could hardly believe it herself, and it looked like he'd taken the breakup pretty hard, by the looks of the beer bottles on the ground.

"I think you're hung over," she said. "Do you want me to get you some coffee?"

"Coffee would be great, but I'm not hung over." He motioned to the ground. "I dumped most of those out so I wouldn't be tempted to get obliterated."

Jane didn't know if she entirely believed him, because he swayed when he stood up from the hammock. She hurried to his side and grasped his arm to steady him.

"Thanks," he said in a quiet voice. "I'm all right—it's just this horrible headache. I can't get it to go away."

"Come inside," Jane said. "I'll make you that coffee. And you should take some aspirin."

Cameron picked up his phone and turned off the music, then slid it into his pocket. In a surprising move, he draped his arm over her shoulder, using her as support. So she walked with him to the deck. They lumbered up the steps, and as they bypassed the shattered glass Jane said, "I'll sweep that up while you're waiting for the coffee."

"No," Cameron said, his voice harsh again. "You're not going to clean up Crystal's mess. I'll do it."

Jane looked up at him, surprised at his vehemence, while trying not to focus on how it felt to have his arm draped over her. "It's all right, really. You should get some rest."

Cameron drew away from her completely. He looked

more steady on his feet, but the pain in his eyes was still there. "I'll be fine, eventually. But you're not sweeping up the glass."

"Okay," Jane said. "I won't sweep up the glass."

Cameron looked relieved. He nodded and walked past her and opened the sliding glass door. Jane followed him inside. She'd grab a trash bag and clean up the food containers and bottles in the yard, but when she took a bag out of the pantry, Cameron held out his hand. "I'll do the yard. You can start on the bedding. I should probably just send you home, since I won't be needing cleaning services anymore. But it would be nice to have all the bedding done at once."

"No problem," Jane assured him, handing over the trash bag. She was glad he wasn't sending her home right away. He wasn't looking too great, and she wanted to keep an eye on him until he at least got some coffee in him.

Jane watched him walk outside, broom, dustpan, and trash bag in hand. She set the coffee maker on, then she went upstairs. She'd cleaned upstairs multiple times, but she always felt like she was intruding when she cleaned a client's bedroom. Mostly she cleaned kitchens and bathrooms, then did floors, and other main parts of houses.

Cameron's bedroom was decidedly masculine, but warm as well. The bedspread was a deep green, and the pillow shams were a quilted, green-and-white pattern—which Jane suspected were hand-stitched. She'd wash them on delicate. She stripped the bedding, dumped it all in the hallway, then went into the other two bedrooms. The bedding in each room was new—she could tell by the stiff feel of the fabric and the sterile scent. Jane was surprised that the beds had been made without laundering the new bedding first. Then Jane remembered Crystal saying something about how they'd been rushed to get ready for the engagement party.

Jane carried two of the sheet sets to the upstairs laundry

room. There was a laundry downstairs as well, which would make everything go twice as fast. She dumped in the sheets, then the pillow cases. She'd wash the comforters in the bigger washer downstairs.

It was strange to think that Cameron and Crystal had called off their wedding. Jane hadn't cared much for Crystal and her prima donna personality, though Jane hadn't wished her this type of ill will. She was curious to know what had happened to break them up, but it was none of her business. Besides, after today, Jane would probably never see either of them again.

She carried the rest of the bedding downstairs. She stopped at the base of the steps when she saw Cameron sitting on one of the couches in the living room, his head in his hands. His cup of coffee was on the table in front of him, untouched, from what she could tell. Jane's heart went out to him. Was he really that devastated over Crystal? Would he try to get back together?

She didn't want to pry more than she already had, so she continued into the kitchen and the second laundry room that was situated between the kitchen and the mud room. She loaded the first comforter into the washer and selected the cycle, then added a detergent pod. With about thirty minutes to wait until she had to change over the laundry, she decided she could at least clean up the kitchen.

She soon found there wasn't much to clean up, so she started to disinfect the sink and counters. No sound came from the living room, where she could see Cameron still sitting on the couch. Should she talk to him? See if there was anything he needed? When another five minutes passed, and he still hadn't moved, Jane wiped her hands off and grabbed a water bottle from the refrigerator. Then she searched the cupboards and found some Advil.

Jane carried it into the living room and sat next to Cameron, leaving a good amount of space between them. She hoped she wasn't being too presumptuous, but it was hard to ignore this man's pain.

He lifted his head as she sat down on the couch.

"Hey," she said. "Here's some water and Advil."

He took both from her wordlessly.

She felt gratified when he drank half the water bottle before setting it down next to the coffee.

He leaned back on the couch and closed his eyes, slowly exhaling.

Jane felt frozen in place. She didn't know if she should ask him how he was doing. Or if she should leave him alone.

"Do you have a boyfriend?" Cameron asked, his eyes still closed.

Jane swallowed. "Not currently." Thoughts of Daniel floated through her mind. They'd been broken up for almost a year, and Jane had been so focused on her dad and her cleaning company that she hadn't really dated since Daniel.

"Have you been married?"

"No."

Cameron cracked an eye open, then closed it again. "So, that last boyfriend you had . . . did you ever take his credit card without asking and buy a houseful of furniture?"

"What?" Jane said. "I . . . *no*. Who would do that?"

Cameron opened his eyes again, his gaze piercing.

"Crystal?"

He nodded.

Jane exhaled. "Wow."

"Yeah. Wow." Cameron pulled out his phone from his pocket. "I took a picture of the invoices that came with the furniture." He turned the phone to face Jane. "Crystal was going to surprise me, she said. Claimed it was my wedding gift. She wanted to replace every bit of furniture in this cabin."

She peered at the list—everything from couches, to tables, to rugs. Then Cameron slid to the next picture, and Jane's mouth fell open when she saw the $35,000 price tag. "You must have a really high limit on your credit card."

Cameron stared at her. Then he started to chuckle. "Yeah, I do, in fact. I would have definitely noticed a $35,000 charge though."

"Plus, the furniture—I mean that would have been noticeable too." Jane waved a hand. "You would have noticed if you came downstairs and didn't have this comfy leather couch to sit on."

"Do you think it's comfortable?" he asked.

Sitting this close to him, she noticed that he'd tamed his hair. It wasn't necessarily brushed, but it wasn't sticking up as it had been before.

"I do." She ran a hand over the soft leather. "It's broken in and has personality."

Cameron's gaze seemed to deepen. "I think so too," he said in a quiet voice. "Do you know my grandfather built this cabin? Well, the original part. The renovations expanded the kitchen, added a second level, and combined the living room and bedroom into one large area."

"But you kept the furniture?"

"Yep," Cameron said, his expression brightening. "I refinished the kitchen table myself."

Jane raised her eyebrows at this and leaned forward to get a view of the table from her position. "That's impressive."

Cameron shook his head. "It took me about as long to do one table as it took the construction crew to do an entire renovation."

"Well, you have a busy job," she said.

"Yeah, that reminds me, I should get to work," Cameron said. "Maybe after a long shower—I need to wake up."

Jane nodded. "Do you want fresh coffee?"

"No, the water was great."

"How about something to eat?" She wasn't hired to cook, but it wouldn't be a problem. "Scrambled eggs will only take a minute."

Cameron looked like he was about to say no. Then he said, "Sure. That would be great."

"Okay, then," Jane said, moving to her feet. "I'll get started."

"I'll get that shower in," Cameron said.

Jane walked to the kitchen, feeling Cameron's gaze on her. It made her feel self-conscious, but she was happy that he seemed to be pulling things together. He'd actually laughed, and she decided that was a good thing.

Twenty minutes later, Cameron came into the kitchen. Jane had gotten more creative than she'd intended. She'd scrambled eggs and heated some pre-cooked bacon she found in the fridge. She added grated cheese and chives to the eggs, hoping he'd like them. She'd also found enough fruit to put together a smoothie.

"This looks great. Are you a chef too?" Cameron said.

"Not exactly," Jane said with a laugh. As he settled at the island, she tried not to ogle him. He wore a button-down shirt, rolled up at the sleeves, and khaki pants. He was still barefoot, and his hair was a bit damp from the shower. And even from her position on the other side of the island, she could smell his freshly showered scent.

Crystal was a fool.

Jane refocused on scrubbing the frying pan. Then she rinsed it off and started to dry it. Cameron seemed to have a pretty healthy appetite after all.

When he caught her watching him, she felt her face heat.

"Do you want some?" he asked.

"Oh, I'm not hungry," Jane said, although she was starting to get hungry—for lunch. "I go home to eat lunch with my dad."

Cameron looked surprised at this. "Every day?"

"Yeah," Jane said, wondering why she was telling him all of this. "I moved here a couple of years ago after his wife died—my stepmom—and I found out his diabetes was pretty severe. I eat with him most meals to ensure that he eats healthy. He can be a bit . . . stubborn."

Cameron nodded. "I definitely understand stubborn.'"

Jane laughed. "That's an understatement."

Five

Cameron continued eating his breakfast-slash-lunch while he listened to Jane talk about her dad. The more he was around Jane, the more impressed he became. She was a hard worker, an entrepreneur, and she was pretty much her dad's caretaker. He also wondered what she'd meant when she'd said she didn't "currently" have a boyfriend.

He didn't have a chance to ask her because someone knocked at the door.

"More furniture?" Jane said.

Cameron narrowed his eyes.

"Too soon?"

"Way too soon," he said but then winked at her. He rose from the stool and walked to the front door. His shower and the food had helped his headache. But when he opened the door, he decided the reprieve might be short lived.

"Mom," Cameron said.

His mom stood on the front porch, wearing golfing clothes, complete with a pink visor. Her arms were folded, and she didn't look happy. "I've been trying to get ahold of you. Why haven't you returned my calls or texts?"

Cameron opened the door wider. "Come in. We need to talk."

His mother's expression changed from stern to worried. "Is everything okay? Whose car is in the driveway?"

"It's Jane's."

His mom's eyes widened.

"She's the cleaning lady Crystal hired."

"Oh." His mom looked toward the kitchen.

"Hello," Jane said as she rinsed out the sink. Her gaze shifted to Cameron's. "I can go upstairs and change over the laundry so you can have some privacy."

Cameron lifted a hand. "Don't leave on my account. You already know most of the story and can probably guess the rest."

"What story?" his mom asked, giving Jane an interested once-over, then focusing again on Cameron.

"Let's sit down," he said and led her to the kitchen table. He sensed Jane's surprise, but Cameron had nothing to hide.

So, while Jane changed the laundry over on both levels of the house, then moved into the living room to dust, he told his mom first about the honeymoon fiasco, and then about the furniture delivery.

"What in the world was Crystal thinking?" his mom asked. "Taking your credit card and charging $35,000 to it? Without your permission? Unbelievable."

Cameron could only nod. He was starting to feel numb again. Seeing the dismay on his mom's face was making this all the more real. Calling off the wedding would also affect his parents. "I thought about pressing charges but decided canceling the wedding would be enough."

"What did she say when you confronted her?" his mom asked.

Cameron sighed. "I texted to ask about my missing credit card, just to see how she'd respond. She said she had a huge surprise for me, and she'd tell me later, but not to worry, she had my credit card in her safekeeping. When she came over last night with takeout, I showed her the invoice I'd taken a picture of." He showed his mom the picture, and she spent several moments studying it.

When she looked up again, there were tears in her eyes. "I'm so sorry, son. I thought Crystal and you were getting along fine, although . . ." She broke off. "It's a shame all the way around, really."

"Although *what*?" Cameron asked.

His mom rubbed the bridge of her nose. "I hadn't planned on saying anything, because I trust your judgment, but since all this happened . . ."

"Tell me, Mom," he said.

"Dad had some misgivings, and frankly, so did I," she said. "At the introduction dinner with Crystal's mom, the woman asked some very personal questions, such as what Dad's net worth is. She also wanted to know if we could hire her brother. Dad said he was happy to do an interview but couldn't guarantee a job. Normally, that wouldn't have been a big deal, but Dad did interview her brother. He has a couple of felonies—did you know that? And he's spent time in prison for embezzlement."

Cameron stared at his mom. "I didn't know. Crystal mentioned her uncle was looking for a job, but we never really talked much more about it. She was probably waiting until we got married to pursue it more."

"We'll probably never know now," his mom said, "but the fact that she took your credit card without you knowing about it worries me. Did you check your statement?"

"Yes, of course," he said. "There was only the $5,000 charge on there. Regardless, I canceled the card, and the company is issuing a new number."

"I'm glad to hear it." His mom lowered her voice. "And how are you doing? I see you're being taken care of this morning." Her brows lifted.

Jane was in the living room. She'd finished dusting and was now spraying glass cleaner on the sliding doors.

"Yeah, Jane is great," he said, keeping his voice low as well. "Crystal hired her, so today will be her last morning. I'm not quite as high maintenance as Crystal is."

"It might be the one good thing Crystal did," his mom said.

"I have no complaints about Jane." He shrugged. "I just don't think I have enough work for her, and I can take out my own trash."

His mom's phone beeped. She took it out and looked at the screen. "Oh, by the way, the reason I came over here was because you hadn't RSVP'd to the hospital gala tonight. It's black tie, you know, but since you own your own tux, that shouldn't be a problem."

Cameron groaned. "I don't think so, Mom. I only crashed in the hammock for a couple of hours before Jane showed up. Plus, everyone will ask why Crystal isn't with me, and then I'll have to explain."

Instead of his mom sympathizing with him, she was smiling. "It will be perfect," she said. "Show up with a different date, and you can get it over with once and for all. There will be some gossip, that's a given. But by tomorrow, it will be simply old news."

"Bring a *date*? You're kidding, right?"

"I'm not kidding," she said. "Unless you want me to suggest to Maryann that you're coming solo. I'm sure she'd be happy to keep you company."

"Maryann Turner?" Cameron rolled his eyes. "What is she on, divorce number five?"

"Six, I think." His mom laughed. "She's always had a soft spot for you, and she's richer than sin."

"She's also old enough to be my mom, no offense. Besides, her fake nails scare me."

His mom kept laughing, then placed a hand on his arm. "You know this charity gala is my baby. I've spent six months organizing it and bringing in *who's who*. If my own son isn't there, that will create even more gossip. Bring a date, have some wine, dance a little, and get into a few bidding wars."

It was really hard to say no to his mom, but Cameron just couldn't stomach the thought of going to the gala less than twenty-four hours after breaking off his engagement. Surely, by now Crystal had told her friends and family and whomever else would listen. He doubted she'd attend the gala herself, since she was going to go with him, and it was MC'd by his mom, but Crystal would have plenty of friends there to report back to her.

"I'll just come for the auction portion," Cameron said. "I won't be able to get a date this late—plus, it would be really awkward trying to explain myself when I'm asked about Crystal."

"Take her," his mom said.

"Crystal?"

"No, *her*." His mom pointed past him.

Cameron looked over his shoulder to see Jane unwinding the cord to the vacuum in the living room. "Jane?"

She switched on the vacuum, and both Cameron and his

mom watched her run the machine back and forth over the carpet. All of a sudden Cameron was imagining what Jane might look like in one of those little black dresses. Maybe with her hair pulled up in a twist. Dangling diamond earrings.

Jane rotated the vacuum and glanced in their direction. She froze. Who could blame her? Both Cameron and his mom were practically staring her down. She switched off the vacuum and gave a tentative smile. "It this too loud?"

"No," his mom answered. "Can you come in here for a moment, though? Cameron has something to ask you."

Cameron felt like a fifteen-year-old boy with all the nerves of asking a girl out when Jane nodded and walked toward them. She smoothed back some strands of hair that had fallen out of her ponytail. Her gaze focused on Cameron, and he noticed she had the lightest sheen of perspiration on her forehead.

"Sure, what is it?" she asked him.

He couldn't believe he was about to give into his mom's request. "We were wondering if you could come to the hospital benefit tonight as our guest."

His mom cleared her throat. "More specifically, as *Cameron's* date."

Jane's eyes widened.

"Not a date, date," Cameron clarified. "More of an escort." He groaned. "That didn't come out right, either."

"What he means is that by not showing up with a date, there will be a lot of speculation and questions," his mom filled in.

"And if he shows up with me, there will be less?" Jane asked.

Cameron looked at his mom. "See? That's exactly what I'm talking about."

Jane took a step back. "I take my dad to the assisted living center on Saturday nights so he can play cards with his friends. It's sort of a tradition."

It was probably true, but Cameron sensed she didn't want to be the center of a gossip storm, or was it because of him personally? He was trying to decide if he should be offended when his mom cut in.

"The gala doesn't start until 8:00 p.m.," his mom said. "The benefit is very important to our family, and Cameron must come. Showing up with a date will tell everyone in Pine Valley that he's moved on from Crystal."

"Mom, she doesn't want to come."

"I don't have anything to wear anyway," Jane said. "Isn't the benefit black tie?"

"I have a closet full of gowns." His mom looked Jane up and down. "You're more busty than I am, and a couple of inches taller, but that shouldn't be too much of a problem."

Cameron's mouth dropped open. "*Mother.*"

She just smiled at him, then turned her appraising gaze to Jane. "Perhaps you can consider it as a job—I'll see to it that Cameron pays you for your time."

Cameron was shocked, and he expected for Jane to be shocked. Instead, she folded her arms. Her gaze darted from Cameron to his mom, then back to him again. "I'm a cleaning lady, *your* cleaning lady. Everyone will know it's some sort of set up."

"She has a point," his mom said, looking at Cameron. "You should ask her properly, then it will be a real date."

Cameron wanted to pull his hair out. Would Jane really agree if he asked her? He eyed her. Her return gaze was steady . . . which was a good sign, he decided. After clearing his throat, he said, "Jane, would you do me the honor of being my date to the hospital gala tonight?"

Jane's mouth quirked, and his pulse hummed. It was a sensation he hadn't expected and couldn't exactly identify.

"I could probably have my neighbor drive my dad back home," she said in a thoughtful tone. "She's always asking to help me with whatever I need."

"Wonderful." His mom clapped her hands together. She stood and leaned toward Cameron, then kissed his cheek. Turning to Jane, his mom said, "Cameron will give you my address, and if you could come around 5:00, we'll pick out something for you to wear."

"All right," Jane said in a faint voice, as if she was just realizing what she'd agreed to.

His mom left before Cameron could get another word in, and moments later, he was facing Jane on his own.

"Are you sure?" he asked Jane, standing up.

She looked at him, and Cameron realized her eyes were more than just dark green. They had gold and brown flecks in them too. "I figured you've had a hard time lately, so I could help you out with this one thing. But seriously, you don't have to pay me."

He held her gaze for a moment. "My mom can be pretty persuasive."

Jane smiled, and Cameron felt his pulse hum again. "I noticed," she said.

He chuckled, feeling lighter somehow. "I really appreciate this. I normally don't have my mom arranging my dates for me, but under the circumstances—"

"It's all right, really," Jane said, moving past him and walking back to the vacuum. "This is important to your family, and I'm in a position to help you out. Don't worry, I know this isn't a real date. Besides, men like you don't date women like me." She flashed him another smile, then turned on the vacuum.

Cameron didn't have a chance to reply; besides, he didn't know exactly what to say.

Six

Jane stared at her reflection in the floor-length mirror at Mrs. Vance's home. She'd tried on a handful of gorgeous gowns, but when she pulled on the red sheath with spaghetti straps, Mrs. Vance had clapped her hands together. "That's the dress! Turn around and look."

She'd been transformed and could see why these types of dresses were so expensive. They did the job well of tucking in and enhancing Jane's figure. The red color made her dark hair gleam, and the soft silk fabric made her feel like she was floating in a warm pool of water.

"It's really beautiful," Jane said. "But it's so . . . red."

Mrs. Vance laughed lightly. "Not everyone can pull off red." She joined Jane at the mirror. "You're young and beautiful. It's all right to flaunt it once in a while."

Jane met Mrs. Vance's gaze in the mirror. "I don't want to stand out."

But Mrs. Vance only winked. "I need to get over to the lodge, and Selena can help you with your hair."

"Selena?"

"She's my assistant, and she's great with hair," Mrs. Vance said. "I told Cameron to pick you up here, since it's on the way to the benefit."

Jane opened her mouth. The red dress was gorgeous, but she didn't like dressing to stand out in a room. But Mrs. Vance was already on her way out of the bedroom suite, calling for Selena.

Maybe Mrs. Vance was right. Tonight Jane could dress like royalty and mingle with the *Who's Who* of Pine Valley. Some were sure to be her clients, but she'd deal with that later. It wasn't like she was living in the eighteenth century when maids didn't socialize with the elite. Although she'd told Cameron that a man like him didn't date a woman like her, she wasn't necessarily referring to their social and financial statuses. His world was so large, whereas her world was very, very small.

"Hello, Jane," a woman said, coming into the bedroom suite. "Louisa said I would find you in here. Oh, goodness. That's a great dress on you."

Jane turned to face a petite, dark-haired woman. "It makes me very nervous, to tell you the truth. I've never worn anything like it."

Selena gave her a sympathetic smile. "No one will ever know." She approached Jane, looking at her with a critical eye. "I think an updo will show off your neck and shoulders. What do you think?"

Jane shrugged. "I trust your judgment. Like I said, this is all new for me. I feel like Cinderella."

Selena had a warm laugh. "Cameron is no prince, mind you. But he is a nice boy. I'm glad he's going tonight. Louisa told me the circumstances."

Jane flushed. She was his charity date—in more ways

than one. But the dress she was wearing would be consolation enough for knowing that her sole purpose at the gala would be as an arm piece. "I'm glad I can help him out. I think in the long run, he'll be better off without Crystal." She bit her lip. "Sorry, I shouldn't have said that."

With a nod, Selena placed her hands on her hips. "I will just say this, and then not bring it up again, but I agree. Cameron would have been miserable with a woman like Crystal. She didn't have an empathetic bone in her body." She moved in front of Jane. "Pearls. You need pearls. Do you have any?"

When Jane shook her head, Selena said, "I'll text Louisa about lending out some of hers." She lifted her hand to stop Jane's protest. "She won't mind, but I need to let her know. Now, let's get you out of that dress and come back here by 7:00 so we can get started on your hair."

"Cameron's coming at 7:30."

"He can wait." Selena's gaze was sly. "You don't want to be early in that dress. Walking in a little late would be more of a statement. What about shoes?"

"I have some black heels."

"Perfect." Selena moved behind Jane and lowered the zipper.

Jane stepped out of the dress and changed back into her clothing while Selena hung up the gown.

"Thank you so much," Jane said when she was ready to leave.

"You're welcome," Selena said with a smile. "This is one of my more enjoyable tasks. All those emails Louisa has me send make me want to stab my eyes out. Now, go. I'll see you at 7:00."

Jane felt practically pushed out the door, but Selena was probably a busy woman. Jane left the elegant home and climbed into her car. Today had been a whirlwind. If she'd imagined this morning the turn of events the day would take, she wouldn't have believed it.

She drove through the wealthy neighborhood, then turned onto the boulevard that would take her to her dad's house. When she pulled up to the small house, her dad was outside, with his cane, watering the flower bed. It was good to see him outside doing yard work; it must be one of his better days.

Jane pulled into the driveway and climbed out of her car. "Hi, Dad," she called loudly enough so he could hear through his earpiece.

He swung around and peered at her through his thick glasses. "You're home late. Did you have a lot of jobs today?"

"No, it was a half day, but some other things came up." She crossed to him and kissed his cheek. "You shaved, and you smell nice."

Her father smiled, his brown eyes twinkling. "It's game day."

Jane grinned. "Right. Let me fix you something to eat, then I'll take you over. Mrs. Sherwood said she'd bring you home. I'm going to a hospital benefit tonight."

"Oh?" He narrowed his eyes. "Why am I just hearing about this now?"

Even though Jane was twenty-seven, her father had no problem treating her like a fifteen- year-old sometimes. "Because I was just invited a short time ago."

"To a five-hundred-dollar-a-plate dinner? That's some invitation."

"I know," Jane said. "I don't have to pay, though. One of my clients had his guest drop out."

"His? Who is this man?" Her father didn't look pleased.

"Don't worry, Dad," she said with a sigh. "It's Cameron

Vance, and it's just business. His mother organized the whole thing, and it was all her idea."

Her dad's brows shot up. "Louisa Vance?"

"Do you know her?" Jane asked.

"She's donated to the assisted living center, that's all," her dad said. He used his cane to walk over to the water spigot and turned it off. Then he bent with a grunt and wound the hose.

Jane knew better than to offer to help him. He was fiercely independent and stubborn. "I'll get your dinner fixed. I'll be eating at the gala," she told him.

"It'd better be worth the money," he said.

Jane smiled. "I don't think it's a meal worth five hundred; most of the money goes to the hospital." She hurried inside and realized she'd been holding her breath. Why her dad's reaction had bothered her, she didn't know.

She busied herself with making a chicken teriyaki meal for her dad with pre-cooked chicken. Then, while it was simmering, she went to her bedroom to find her shoes. She hadn't worn her black heels in a while, and she didn't realize how scuffed they were. So she grabbed a rag and buffed them out with a bit of Vaseline. She hoped no one would pay too much attention to them.

She heard her dad come inside with his distinctive shuffle and turn the TV on in the kitchen. Some news program blared, and Jane sighed. He kept the TV on high volume when he was watching it, and the sound irritated her, but there was no use asking him to turn it down.

Jane found a bag and put the heels in it, along with several makeup items, then went into the front room. She left the bag next to the door and joined her dad in the kitchen.

"Smells good," he said from where he sat at the kitchen table, facing the TV on the end of the counter.

Jane checked on the meal, stirred it, then turned down

the heat. She fixed a glass of ice water and set it on the table along with a plate and utensils.

"You need to watch out for people like the Vances," her dad suddenly said over the volume of the TV. "They're uppity."

Jane turned to look at him. "They're actually nice people." She'd seen a whole different side to Cameron the past couple of days, and even though he was wealthy, there were worse flaws than that. Like Crystal-type flaws.

Her father shook his head, but he remained silent until Jane served the food. She sat across from him and watched the news. The weather report had just come on.

"Looks like it's going to rain," her dad said. "Take a jacket with you."

Jane almost rolled her eyes at the thought of wearing one of her old jackets over the thousand-dollar red dress. "I'll be inside the whole night."

"You don't want to catch a chill," her dad said, his gaze sliding to hers.

Jane appreciated the concern, but again, she was a grown woman. "I'll be sure to keep an eye on the weather."

The next hour passed agonizingly slowly as her dad continued to make comments about the Vances and Jane straightened up around the house. Finally, it was time to take her dad to his game night. Jane usually went with him and enjoyed playing at one of the tables with the residents. Her dad's friend, Pete Southerland, was a character and always made her laugh.

The drive to the center was only a few minutes, and as they arrived, rain started to sprinkle on the car's windshield.

"I told you it was going to rain," her dad said as she handed him his cane after opening his car door.

She pursed her lips together and walked with him into

the center. Once they were inside the gathering room, and the residents found out she wasn't going to stay, Jane almost regretted accepting the invitation to the gala. Pete Southerland always joked with her, and several of the other residents had become dear to her.

"I'll be back next week," she told Pete, squeezing his hand.

She left and hurried out into the rain. It was coming down pretty hard now. She drove straight to Mrs. Vance's home and parked in the circular driveway, hoping she'd be out of the way of any other cars that might come and go that night. Cameron would be picking her up here at 7:30, but Jane failed to see how she'd be completely ready by then.

Selena answered the door. "What a night," she said when she saw Jane on the front porch. "Come in out of the rain." She scanned Jane's hair. "Good, you're not too wet. Some dampness might work to our advantage."

"I don't have a jacket that will go with the dress," Jane said. "Do you have one of those large umbrellas?" She'd hate to get any water damage on the dress.

"You can borrow Mrs. Vance's wrap if it's still raining when Cameron comes," Selena said, leading the way up the curved staircase. "We have plenty of those golf umbrellas."

"Okay, great," Jane said as they headed along the upper hallway. "I just don't want to ruin the dress."

"A little rain won't hurt it, but you don't have to worry." Selena opened the door to the bedroom suite. "These gowns are more sturdy than you think."

Jane walked into the suite and started to undress as Selena fetched the dress. With a little help, Jane was wearing the dress in a few minutes.

"Have a seat at the vanity table," Selena said and produced a large velvet jewelry box. "Mrs. Vance said you're welcome to wear her pearls tonight. I think it will be just the thing."

She opened the box, and Jane stared at the lustrous pearls. They were beautiful.

Selena swept back Jane's hair and brushed it smooth, then pinned it into a French twist. When Selena had secured the pearl necklace, and Jane had put on the pearl earrings, Selena stepped aside. "Come to the mirrors to see what you think. Did you bring your shoes?"

Jane pointed to the bag she brought with her, and Selena went to pull them out. She handed them over to Jane, who slipped them on and turned toward the mirror.

"What do you think?" Selena asked.

Jane wasn't sure she knew the woman in the mirror. "I don't think anyone will be recognizing me."

Selena gave a soft laugh. "Perhaps not, but they'll certainly be noticing you."

Jane bit her lip. "I'm not sure I want that."

Selena turned back to Jane's bag and pulled out her makeup pouch. "I'll leave you to do your makeup. I'm going to slip on my dress too."

"Are you going to the gala?"

"In an official capacity," Selena said. "I'll be running the credit card machine for the winning bidders. You won't even notice me in the background."

"Thank you for everything." Jane spread her hands. "I couldn't have done all this without your help."

Selena smiled. "You're most welcome."

Seven

Cameron was nearly twenty minutes late pulling up to his mom's house. He snatched the umbrella from his back seat he'd stored there before leaving his house and hopped out of his car. He'd been wondering all afternoon which dress Jane would borrow from his mom. He probably shouldn't be wondering about such a thing, but it was better than berating himself for all the time he'd wasted with Crystal over the past few months.

It was strange not having her calling or texting him every moment, hovering, demanding. *Peace.* That's what he was feeling for the first time in a long time. It didn't mean that his work stress was gone, but he was no longer facing huge events like the wedding, honeymoon, and setting up house with Crystal. He could get back to the old Cameron. The one who used to enjoy life.

Still, after his mom and Jane had left his house, Cameron had second thoughts about taking Jane to the gala. It might give off the perception that he was a player, and he didn't need that image to interfere with the hospital benefit. Or at least people thinking that he was callous and already dating right after his canceled engagement. So he'd called his mom, but she was adamant about him keeping the obligation with Jane.

"There's no harm in bringing a date to the gala. Besides, everything isn't always about you," his mom had said. "You're supporting your mother and the community. And you should see Jane in the dress she picked out. Canceling on her would be discourteous."

Cameron had sighed and hung up with his mom. Moments later, Crystal had sent a rather nasty text, basically threatening him that if he told anyone about the furniture purchase she'd made, she'd find a way to discredit him. Cameron had spoken too soon . . . apparently he wasn't going to have peace quite yet. Crystal was a cunning woman.

He'd texted back that only his parents knew, but they wouldn't share it. This wasn't entirely the truth, but if Crystal knew his parents were aware of the fraud, it might keep her on better behavior.

Cameron opened his parents' front door with his key, and as he stepped inside the entrance, he wondered if he should have knocked or rung the doorbell first. Now it was too late.

"There you are," Selena said, coming out of the kitchen. She was dressed in a classy navy suit, with a Bluetooth at her ear. "Oh, good, you brought an umbrella. Jane was worried about ruining her dress."

Cameron looked over at the living room. "Where is Jane?" Since he was late, he fully expected her to be waiting.

"I'll get her," Selena said and started up the stairs.

Cameron hoped that Jane wasn't one of those women who kept a date waiting for an hour.

But he didn't have to worry, because moments after Selena disappeared from the landing, another woman appeared at the top of the stairs.

Cameron stared as Jane walked down the steps. His mom had been right. Canceling on Jane would have been very discourteous. She wore a fitted red dress, accentuating the curves Cameron had only guessed at when she'd worn her jeans and T-shirts to clean in—not that he was admitting to guessing at anything. Her hair was done up, leaving her shoulders bare. The pearls she wore seemed to gleam beneath the glow of the chandelier.

Cameron swallowed.

"You brought an umbrella," she said.

Cameron held it up stupidly as if to say, yes, he had brought an umbrella that they could both plainly see. "It's still raining," he said.

She had neared the final step, and Cameron instinctively held his hand out. Jane placed her hand in his as she stepped down the final stair and came to stand before him. She smelled like summer blossoms, and he noticed she wore dark red lip gloss, which complemented her dress very nicely. This gown couldn't be his mother's—or if it was, he'd never seen her wear it.

"What do you think?" Jane asked in a soft voice.

Cameron blinked, then realized he was still holding her hand. He released it and said, "You're stunning, Jane." Perhaps that wasn't the right thing to say . . . In this circumstance, he should be more professional and cordial.

Her rosy lips turned up in a smile. "You clean up well too, Mr. Vance."

"Cameron, remember?" he said.

She nodded, making her teardrop pearl earrings sway. "I remember."

"Don't forget your wrap," Selena came down the stairs, carrying a black wrap. She set it on Jane's shoulders with a smile. "I'll see you there."

"Thank you," Jane told Selena, then turned back to Cameron.

He realized he was still staring at her. Forcing himself to walk, he crossed to the door and opened it. The rain had lightened up, but he popped open the umbrella and guided Jane to the car. Opening the passenger door for her, he made sure to keep the umbrella over her as she climbed in. Then he hurried around to the other side of the car, folded the umbrella, then set the dripping thing on the floor behind his seat.

He didn't know why his heart was racing after such a short jaunt to the car. He tried to calm his breathing so Jane wouldn't notice as he started the engine. "Did you get your dad off to his game night okay?" he asked.

Jane looked over at him. "Yes, although Pete wasn't too happy."

"Pete? Your dad?"

"Oh, no." She gave a small laugh. "He's the friend my dad visits. They go way back. I think Pete has a bit of a crush on me, although I keep telling him I'm too young for someone as classy as he."

Cameron chuckled. He didn't doubt that this Pete fellow had a crush on Jane. She was easy to talk to, not to mention beautiful. "So . . . uh . . . Do you spend every Saturday night there?"

"Yep," Jane said, and he heard warmth in her voice. "The people at the center are so interesting to talk to. Their life stories are remarkable, and they're also full of wisdom. If I ever have a question or problem, they're quick to give advice, even unsolicited."

"Like Facebook gives advice?"

Jane laughed. "That's one way to put it. I prefer talking to people in person."

"Me too." Cameron turned onto the street that led to the Pine Valley Ski Resort. The benefit would take place at the Alpine Lodge restaurant. He glanced over at Jane and saw that she was watching him.

"Did you get some sleep?" she asked. "You're looking much better—not that a tux doesn't help a man look better."

He smirked. "A tux does help, but yeah, I did crash for about an hour."

"I'm glad," she said. "I didn't want my charity date falling asleep on me."

"Charity? Is that what I am?" he teased, stealing a glance at her.

"*I'm* the charity date," Jane said. "But I don't mind. It's not every day a girl gets to wear a dress like this. I'm just afraid to eat anything. I don't want to get it dirty."

"I'm afraid you'll have to eat—it's five hundred a plate, you know."

"Yeah, my dad told me." She sighed. "Maybe I could ask for a to-go box."

Cameron laughed. "I dare you."

Jane shook her head. "I don't think I'm that brave. Besides, I am pretty hungry, and it probably beats the chicken teriyaki I fixed for my dad earlier."

"I don't know about that," Cameron said. "I happen to know you're a pretty good cook."

She smiled. "I can hold my own."

"Hmm," Cameron mused. "You'll have to let me know if the Alpine Lodge meal passes your muster. Have you eaten there before?"

"Not yet," she said. "Like I mentioned, my weekends are filled with work and playing card games with senior citizens."

Lights glowed from the Alpine Lodge as they turned into the parking lot, and Cameron pulled into the line of cars waiting for valet service. "Maybe someday I'll check out the center. I've been known to win a few card games."

"They don't play for money, you know," she said in a teasing tone. "You'll have to bring your own package of butterscotch candy."

"Sounds good to me." Cameron pulled forward; there were two cars ahead of them. He looked over at her. "Hey, before we go into the gala, I want to thank you for agreeing to come tonight. I know it was last minute—"

"No problem." Jane lifted a hand to cut him off. "And don't you dare offer me money again. Your mom tried multiple times. I'm happy to play Cinderella for one night. I just hope you won't get any backlash from Crystal later."

"Don't worry about that," Cameron said. "She's already texted me a few threats today. I might see if I can snag my lawyer friend Dawson Harris while we're here and show the texts to him."

Jane's brows shot up. "What did she threaten?"

"Nothing specific—just to cause trouble if I tell anyone about the furniture purchases," he said.

A valet approached the car.

"Well, here we go." Cameron put the car into park. They were under the hotel awning, so he didn't need to worry about using the umbrella to get Jane inside the building. He hurried around the car again and opened her door.

She placed her hand in his as she climbed out of the car. Yep, she smelled like summer blossoms. Cameron moved her hand to the crook of his elbow. But then she turned and set the wrap she'd been wearing on the front seat of the car.

Cameron was more than aware of her warmth on his arm as they walked to the front entrance. They were greeted by the director of the hospital, who had taken it upon himself to welcome every guest who entered the building. The director didn't look surprised to see Cameron with a woman who wasn't Crystal, so Cameron surmised that his mom had told the man about the breakup.

The inside of the building had been decorated to look like a scene out of Shakespeare's *A Midsummer Night's Dream*, with huge potted plants and billowing streamers flowing down from the ceiling. The benefit's theme for the night was printed on a giant banner that read "Give the Dream of a Healthy Life."

In the main lobby, several tables were set up with auction items, and a young woman dressed in a fairy costume approached them with an auction number.

"Are you together, or would you like your own numbers?" she asked.

"We're together," Cameron was quick to say. He didn't want Jane worrying about bidding on an item.

The costumed woman handed over the auction number.

"Thank you," Cameron said and took the number.

"What are your names, and I can tell you your dinner table number."

Cameron gave her his name while he glanced about. Several people milled about the tables, and a band played soft jazz music in the main restaurant beyond.

"This place looks amazing," Jane said, sounding truly impressed. "Did your mom orchestrate the decorations as well?"

"She did," he said. "She's been working on the details for months."

"No wonder she didn't want you to miss this."

Cameron laughed. "I think she's got you on her side already." He paused when he saw a man at the far table turn. "Come on, there's my father. I'll introduce you."

He crossed to his dad and introduced him to Jane.

"Nice to meet you, young lady," his dad said, giving her hand a hearty shake. Then he leaned close to Cameron. "Are you doing all right? Your mother told me what happened, but all my calls went to voicemail."

"I turned off my phone for a while, but I'm fine," Cameron said. "Actually, better than fine."

His dad's gaze shifted to Jane, then back to Cameron. There was a mischievous gleam in his eyes. "You look better than I thought you would. Your mother gave me strict orders to keep an eye on you, but I think you're in good hands."

"Oh, there's Mr. Richardson," Cameron said, trying to distract his dad from saying anything that might be overheard by other guests. It worked.

"I'll catch up with you later," his dad said and moved past them to talk to his friend.

"Sorry about that," Cameron said, turning to Jane. "My dad is a great businessman, but sometimes he can be a bit goofy."

Jane smiled. "I don't mind."

They walked past a couple of auction items. "Anything catch your eye?" he asked.

Jane looked at him, her green eyes reflecting the glow from the lights about the room. "Are we shopping?"

He chuckled. "In a manner of speaking. But no golf packages."

"You don't like golf?" Jane asked as they stopped in front of a basket filled with golf balls and a certificate for a game of four.

"I do, but that's how I met Crystal—we both bid on the

same golf package at a charity event." He shrugged. "I conceded after a few bidding rounds, and she invited me to join her. She's actually a terrible golfer, so I should have seen that as a red flag. Why would someone who couldn't golf bid on a package?"

"To get a date with you?" Jane said.

"It was clever, I guess."

Jane stepped closer and looked down at the certificate. "Sounds like a nice package. Do you think some of these are recycled? I mean, the auction items are so similar at these events, not that I've been to a ton of them."

"Oh, I'm sure some of them are," Cameron said, pointing at a football that was signed by an NFL player. "I've seen that football at least three times."

Jane laughed. "I guess if it's all in the name of charity, it works."

"Especially this one," he said, and they continued to move along the table, looking at the auction items. "What about this Blendtec? Do you need one?"

"No," Jane said. "My mom has one, and it sounds like a giant train is plowing through the house when you turn it on."

"Good to know," Cameron said. "What about the Hawaii vacation?"

"That would be amazing," Jane said. "But it's a little forward for a second date."

Cameron smirked. "Ah," he said, eyeing the next item. "This is more my style." The gift basket included gourmet food items. "I'll be snacking until Christmas."

"Sounds good to me," Jane said. "I love flavored honey."

"I'll keep that in mind." They stopped in front of another golf package. "I just can't get away from these."

She laughed. "I should probably let you know that I was on my high school's golf team."

"Really?" Cameron looked down at her. "That's impressive."

"Not exactly," Jane said with a shrug. "Only one girl was even good enough to shoot below 80 consistently. I think my best was 82."

"That's decent . . ."

Jane narrowed her eyes. "You'd better not say, 'for a girl.'"

He laughed. "I wasn't going to."

She shoved him in his arm, and he raised his hands. "I promise, I wasn't going to say that."

"I don't believe you for a moment," Jane said.

"You two are sure enjoying the evening," a woman said, coming to stand on the other side of Cameron.

He looked over to see Lacey, a friend of Crystal's, and the travel agent Crystal had been in cahoots with. She was a tall, willowy woman, and her eyes seemed to shoot daggers at Cameron. He knew he'd run into people who knew Crystal, he just didn't expect it to be someone so directly involved.

"Have we met?" Lacey asked, her daggers going to Jane.

Eight

The woman glaring at Jane could have frozen Florida with her eyes.

"I'm Jane Morris," she said, sticking out her hand.

The woman hesitated, then extended her hand. Yep, her hands were as cold as her personality.

"I'm Lacey. Crystal and I are best friends."

Jane ignored the Crystal remark, although she practically heard Cameron grinding his teeth. "Nice to meet you," Jane said in a cheerful tone because she suddenly wanted to irritate this Lacey person as much as possible. What she really wanted to say was, "Do you buy furniture with stolen credit cards too?"

Lacey was still staring at her, as if she were trying to place Jane. But they'd never met before. Jane had no doubt, however, that seconds after they parted ways Lacey would be texting Crystal and would find out that Jane was the cleaning lady.

"I hope you enjoy the evening," Cameron told Lacey, obviously trying to end the conversation. He placed a hand on Jane's elbow and steered her to the next table over.

But Lacey followed. "The deposit you made for your honeymoon didn't clear. It said the credit card was denied. I require a nonrefundable deposit with every booking even if the booking is canceled. It reimburses me for my time investment."

Cameron stopped and slowly turned to Lacey. "This isn't the time or the place."

Lacey's lips twitched. "Don't think you can stiff me, Cameron Vance. Grooms pay for the honeymoon."

"I'm not trying to stiff anyone," he said, his voice dead calm. "I'll call you tomorrow."

Lacey lifted her chin, staring at Cameron. Jane realized she was holding her own breath. *Back down,* she wanted to tell Lacey. The auction area was getting crowded, and more than one person had glanced over at them.

"If you don't pay the nonrefundable deposit, I'll have to go through legal channels," Lacey said in a hard voice.

Cameron lifted one of his brows as he met her gaze, but said nothing else.

After a tense moment, Lacey puffed out a breath, then turned and walked away.

"Come on," Cameron said, grasping Jane's hand. He led her in the opposite direction that Lacey had gone.

Jane was stunned at Lacey's audacity. Were these really the type of people Cameron associated with? Cameron was gripping her hand like he was a small child crossing a busy street with his mom, so she wasn't about to question him right now. He greeted several people in a brisk tone on the way to their table.

Once they reached the table, Cameron pulled out a chair for her, but she could tell his thoughts were a million miles away. He took a seat next to her and pulled out his phone. He spent the next several minutes texting someone, so Jane didn't say anything. She watched people mill about, greeting each other, laughing, talking, hugging.

Jane felt her heart tug toward Cameron as he sat in his small world of pain and frustration. She reached for the crystal water glass that was a part of the elegant place setting and filled it with ice water from the pitcher. She filled Cameron's glass as well.

"Thanks," he said, coming out of his fog. He swallowed down some water. "Sorry about Lacey. I'm sure the deposit isn't very much, but the way she approached me was irritating. And she was rude to you."

"Don't worry about her," Jane said. "She's just sticking up for her friend. Besides, I don't want you to spend the night apologizing to me."

Cameron nodded. His gaze flitted over her face, and Jane wondered if she'd smeared her lipstick or anything.

"I need to make one more apology," he said.

Jane lifted her brows, trying not to smile.

"I'm not myself," he said. "Breaking the engagement was absolutely the right decision, but now I'm questioning my judgment on many things over the last few months. I'm sorry that you're in the middle of this firestorm when this should be an enjoyable evening."

Jane opened her mouth to contradict him, but he held up his hand.

"I don't know what else this evening has in store," he continued, "but I would be a poor date if I didn't ask you to dance."

He was asking her to dance? Right now? She glanced over at the dance floor. The band was playing, but no one was dancing. "Now?" she asked, turning back look at him.

"After dinner."

"Oh," she said, her face warming. "That's a relief."

He smiled, and she felt relieved that he could smile at all.

"Here's the invoice," a woman said above them. Lacey had returned, and she slapped a piece of paper on the table in front of Cameron.

Jane stared at it in disbelief. Cameron was more quick to recover. He picked it up, and Jane could clearly see that the deposit was $450.00.

"I thought we decided to talk about this tomorrow," he said without looking at Lacey.

She folded her arms. "I don't know if I trust you to follow up on that, so I decided to hand deliver it."

"You had the invoice with you?" Cameron said.

"It was in my car."

Jane noticed that Lacey looked as if she'd gotten sprinkled on by the rain.

"Cash or check?" Cameron asked.

"Preferably cash, since I don't really trust a check from you after what happened with the credit card," Lacey said.

Jane wanted to tell Lacey exactly why Cameron had to cancel his card, but it wasn't her place.

"All right," Cameron said, standing up. He reached into his tuxedo jacket pocket and pulled out a thin wallet.

Jane watched as he counted out a series of fifty-dollar bills and handed over the invoice amount to Lacey.

"Four hundred fifty in cash," Cameron said, then tore the invoice in half, and half again. He handed the ripped pieces to Lacey. "Deposit paid. I hope you enjoy the evening." He turned to Jane and held out his hand.

She placed it in his and rose to her feet.

"Let's go say hello to my mom," Cameron said.

Jane nodded, and Lacey practically stalked away, gripping the fifty-dollar bills in her cold hands.

Cameron dropped Jane's hand and motioned her to walk in front of him. "She's over there by Selena."

"Oh, I see them," Jane said, catching sight of the two women standing near the doors that led to the terrace. She looked back at Cameron. "Do you always carry so much cash with you?"

"I planned to tip some of the workers here tonight," he said. "They donate their time to help with the benefit so that there's very little overhead."

Jane didn't have time to reply, because Cameron's mom had spotted them and waved them over. She was all smiles when they approached.

"You look wonderful," she said to Jane. "Your date looks all right too."

Cameron leaned down and kissed his mom's cheek. "Everything seems to be running smoothly," he said. "You've brought in quite the crowd."

"I have Selena to thank for that," his mom said. "She was like a pit bull getting all the RSVPs secured."

Selena winked at Jane. "Just doing my job, Louisa."

"Are you two enjoying yourselves?" his mom asked. Although she was smiling, Jane knew the question carried weight.

"We ran into Crystal's travel agent, but I don't think she'll be bothering me anymore." Cameron grabbed an hors d'oeuvre from a passing waiter carrying a tray. "Do you want anything, Jane?"

"Maybe later," she said, impressed at how quickly he

could switch from complimenting his mom's event, to talking about Lacey, to asking Jane if she wanted something.

Cameron took a bite of what looked like a mini chicken wrap. "Mmm. This is excellent." He finished it off in one more bite. "You should really try it."

Before Jane could protest, he called over the waiter, and with everyone watching, Jane picked up the chicken wrap, holding a napkin beneath it to protect her dress. She took a bite and chewed. It was delicious.

"Do you like it?" Cameron asked, watching her with interest.

Jane wasn't entirely used to a guy like Cameron, or any guy for that matter, intently watching her eating.

"It's good, really good," she said, then caught his mom watching both of them with interest.

"Great." Cameron grinned. "I was afraid you were a vegetarian or something."

"No way." Jane glanced quickly at his mom and Selena. "Not that there's anything wrong with being a vegetarian."

His mom just laughed. "We're not vegetarians either. But Crystal is, and she was quick to complain at functions like this if special dietary meals weren't to her liking."

"Oh," Jane said, and exhaled. "Well, I'm not picky, which will probably catch up with my waistline one day."

Another waiter approached with a tray of shrimp appetizers. Jane didn't hesitate to help herself this time.

"Have you seen your father?" Cameron's mom asked him. "He's supposed to be hosting the auctioneer, Mr. Broadbent, but I see Mr. Broadbent sitting at the table by himself."

"We'll go and speak with him while you find Dad," Cameron said.

"Bless you, son," his mom said, and the two shared a smile.

Jane nearly sighed aloud. Cameron might have had a terrible fiancée, but he had great parents. In Jane's opinion, that could make up for a lot.

Nine

The more time Cameron spent with Jane, the more he forgot Crystal. And the more he wondered how he could have ever spent more than a few minutes with his ex-fiancée. Jane was everything Crystal wasn't, and other people at the benefit were taking notice. Sweet, genuine, charming, intelligent, witty . . . that was Jane. If Cameron had come alone, he knew he wouldn't have been greeted by so many of the guests—they were simply curious about Jane.

And once they met her, a few nodded their approval.

It was a heady feeling.

Except, Jane wasn't his girlfriend. The date was just an arrangement, and she didn't seem to treat him with any special interest above anyone else. Perhaps that was her charm. She became instant best friends with whomever she met, within two minutes of meeting them. And Cameron had been drawn in as well.

He must be on the rebound something fierce since all he wanted to do was keep Jane to himself and dance with her. No interruptions from anyone else. But the dancing was still a way off. Dinner was winding down, and Cameron had truly enjoyed watching Jane enjoy her food. She was definitely a foodie, which he found inordinate pleasure in.

The auction started out with gusto, and Cameron bid on a few things but didn't get too aggressive until one of the baskets of gourmet food that included flavored honey came up for bid. He raised his number as the auctioneer requested a bid for one hundred dollars.

Jane turned to him. "You really don't have to."

He leaned toward her, catching the summer-blossom scent that had been plaguing him all night. "I like flavored honey too."

She rolled her eyes but was smiling as she settled back in her chair.

He kept raising his number as the auctioneer drove the price. After $300, it was down to Cameron and his friend Dawson Harris bidding. Cameron caught Dawson's smirk, and that only made Cameron bid higher. When it reached $625, Dawson finally caved.

"Sold!"

Cameron had won the basket, and he looked over at Jane in triumph. She was covering her mouth in disbelief. "It had better be good," he said as the auctioneer rattled off the next item.

"Six twenty-five is crazy for a basket of honey," she said, her eyes gleaming with amusement.

"I couldn't let Dawson outbid me."

"Who's Dawson?" Jane asked.

"A business associate who's also a lawyer," he said. "He's helped my dad with a few things."

Cameron hadn't missed Dawson eying Jane from across

the room, and that had only added more fuel to Cameron's incentive to win the bid.

And . . . here came Jeff Finch, the realtor. The man was one of those guys who seemed to attract women wherever he went. And Cameron really shouldn't be surprised he was curious about Jane. The last item had been auctioned off, and people had started to rise from the tables. Some would leave now; others would stay for the dancing.

"Cameron, I'm on my way out, but I wanted to say hi first," Jeff said, arriving at their table and reaching out to shake Cameron's hand.

"Nice to see you," Cameron said. "This is Jane. You might remember her from the engagement party the other night."

Jeff shook her hand as well.

"Jeff's a local realtor," Cameron supplied.

"I've seen your advertising," Jane said with a smile. "I think the entire population of Pine Valley knows who you are."

Jeff chuckled. "Well, thank you. Nice meeting you, and we'll catch up later, Cameron."

Cameron ignored the significant look Jeff threw at him. As Jeff walked away from the gala, Jane released an audible sigh. Cameron looked over at her. "Are you all right?"

"It's just that your female friends glare at me, and your male friends are all smiles," she said. "What's up with that?"

"Do I need to explain the birds and the bees to you?" He felt guilty when she blushed, but only a little. He propped his elbows on the table and leaned close. "It's all part of the singles game, you know."

Her mouth quirked. "You mean if I didn't spend my Saturday nights playing cards with eighty-year-old men, I'd be a little more aware of the jungle out there?"

"I wouldn't exactly call it a jungle, more like a wilderness. With no water."

When Jane's brows arched in question, he clarified. "You, in that red dress, are like an oasis in a vast desert."

"Hmm." She linked her fingers together on the table top. "I think I'm more of a mirage. I could never afford a dress like this, not to mention the tickets to the gala, or the $625 gourmet basket."

"Good thing I didn't bring you for your money, then," Cameron said, grinning at her.

This produced another blush.

"How about that dance, and then we can get out of here?" He stood and held out his hand. She put her hand in his and rose to her feet. As they walked to the dance floor, he could feel people watching them. They were still holding hands, which might make people think they were involved. But he suddenly didn't care what the other guests thought, or if they were talking about his canceled engagement.

He had a beautiful woman to dance with; then he'd take her home, and the night would be over. He might as well enjoy this moment, because tomorrow he had to start cleaning up all the messes he'd made of his life. He wasn't looking forward to canceling the bookings Crystal had set up for the wedding. She'd told him that since he was the one who wanted to break up, he could do the work of canceling everything. Who knew how many other nonrefundable deposits were out there?

The band was playing a slow melody by the time they reached the floor, and Cameron turned to Jane, putting one hand on her waist and keeping her other hand in his. She rested her free hand on his shoulder. The lights dimmed, and a machine on the bandstand threw images of stars and tiny moons all over the ceiling and floor.

"I feel like everyone is staring," Jane said, "but when I

look at their faces, no one is actually looking. Maybe it's a trick of the light?"

"These people are a sly bunch. They can avert their eyes really quickly."

Jane laughed.

And Cameron felt the vibration of her laughter travel through his own body. He was probably enjoying this evening much more than he should. He hadn't seen Lacey since he'd given her the money, but he had no doubt he'd have a message or a text from Crystal once he turned his phone back on. He couldn't imagine Crystal staying silent when she found out his date tonight was their cleaning lady.

A cleaning lady who cleaned up very nicely.

"What are you smiling about?" Jane asked, her green eyes connecting with his.

"Just . . . random thoughts."

"Hmm," Jane said, pressing her rosy lips together. She must have reapplied her lip gloss when he wasn't looking. "What's the saying? Penny for your thoughts?"

Cameron liked how Jane's eyelashes were long without being fake. "What?"

"You have selective hearing like my dad."

"All right, all right," he said. "I was thinking about how furious Lacey was when she obviously doesn't know the story behind my canceled credit card. Then I thought how I haven't seen her since I gave her the cash. And I realized she probably texted Crystal all about it, not knowing that Crystal would also know the truth behind the canceled credit card. Also, Lacey wouldn't waste any time telling her about *you*."

Jane watched him in amusement. "Those are a lot of random thoughts."

"I'm not finished."

"Well then, please continue."

He smirked. "I turned my phone off, but I'm betting myself Crystal has sent several scathing texts calling me out on bringing a date to the gala so soon after our breakup."

"And," Jane prompted, "you forgot to add to your random thoughts that Crystal will be really annoyed your date is her cleaning lady."

"*Ex*-cleaning lady." Cameron shrugged. "What does it matter? The real issue is that Crystal can't complain about what I do anymore. We're not together."

"True." She glanced past him. "The band is actually quite good."

"Um-hmm," Cameron said and then realized he'd pulled Jane a little closer during their conversation, and she hadn't seemed to mind.

The number came to an end, and Jane used her free hand to cover up a yawn. "Sorry, I don't mean to yawn around you. Besides, I'm sure you're way more tired than I am."

"I didn't have to clean houses today like you did," Cameron said as the band started playing another slow song. "If you're tired, we can go. No problem. Or . . . we could dance one more."

Jane smiled. "One more is fine, but only if you want to."

Cameron's answer was to pull her just a little closer and keep dancing. More couples were on the dance floor now, but the dim lighting gave them some anonymity. The dance was over way too soon, and Cameron felt like he was waking up from a deep dream when Jane drew away from him.

"Let's say goodbye to my mom. Then we can pick up your basket," Cameron said.

She lifted a brow. "You mean *your* basket?"

"Nope. It's yours."

Jane bit her lip, and Cameron touched her arm. "It's for

charity, remember? Maybe I'll take one of the honeys, but you can have the rest. Share it with your dad."

Finally, she nodded. "All right. He'll be so impressed."

It took only a moment to locate his mom, who happened to be dancing with his dad. Cameron said his goodbyes. His dad gave Jane's hand an enthusiastic shake, and his mom said, "I'm so glad you could come, Jane."

They made it out of the restaurant with only a few more stops, including picking up the gourmet food basket, and by the time they stepped out into the summer night, Cameron was glad to be free of all the people.

"It's stopped raining," Jane said as they waited for the valet to bring the car.

Cameron shifted the basket he held to his other arm; it was heavier than he expected. "I love the smell after it rains."

"I was just going to say that," she said, looking over at him with a smile.

Cameron smiled back, but he noticed that her smile seemed less happy now. "Did you enjoy the night?"

"Very much," she said. "Thank you for taking me. I need to do something for your mom to thank her for loaning me this dress."

"I don't think you have to worry about that," he said. "She was happy to do it."

The breeze stirred about them, bringing with it the fresh scent of earth and leaves.

"Are you cold?" Cameron asked.

She gave a small shake of her head, which dislodged a lock of hair from her updo. "I'm fine."

Cameron lifted his hand and tucked her hair back in, feeling Jane's gaze on him. Just then the valet pulled up with his car, and Cameron dropped his hand.

While the valet hopped out, Cameron opened the passenger door for Jane.

She picked up the wrap from the front seat where she'd left it, then sat down.

Cameron shut her door and put the basket in the back seat. He paid the valet and walked around to the other side.

The drive home was quiet, although they talked about a couple of random things. But the mood definitely changed and become more somber. Jane checked her phone and reported that her dad had made it home all right and had probably gone to bed by now.

When Cameron pulled up to his mom's house to drop Jane off, she said, "It was a great evening. Thanks again, Cameron."

He tried not to focus on the soft way she said his name. "I'm glad you agreed to come." And here it was, the awkward part of knowing what to say next. Their date was pretty much a convenient arrangement, yet Cameron didn't want to tell her goodbye and never see her again. But what else could he say— *Can I hire you? Do you want to go to dinner sometime?*

For whatever reason, he was coming up empty. Probably because he wanted to skip past all the awkwardness, ignore the fact that he was probably on the rebound, and kiss her anyway.

Ten

Jane waited as Cameron came around the car to open the door for her. She probably should have just opened it herself, but she technically needed his help to stand while wearing the form-fitting red dress.

He'd been a gentleman all night, even when confronted by Lacey. Jane had been impressed—more than impressed. Cameron Vance wasn't the man she had first thought he was. She supposed she was guilty of stereotyping him simply because he was wealthy. She should know better, but money had never been a simple thing for her.

She'd always had to work hard to keep a roof overhead, and even though she was living with her dad rent-free right now, she was paying half of all utilities and repairs to the house, as well as secretly paying some of his medical expenses, while putting money into savings each month. She hoped to expand her business and hire on a part-time helper, especially since she was often cleaning until 6:00 or 7:00 p.m. at night.

The door opened, and Cameron offered his hand, just as she knew he would.

Jane stood, her hand in Cameron's warm, sturdy one.

Cameron was right. The fresh air after the rain storm smelled wonderful, and when she got home, she'd probably sit on the back porch for a while. She wanted to remember every bit of the evening, with the exception of the Lacey confrontation.

Cameron dropped her hand and opened the rear door to fetch the basket. "I'll carry it in for you," he said.

They walked to the porch. Jane felt awkward since this wasn't her house, and this wasn't really a date, and she was wearing Cameron's mom's dress. She was both relieved and disappointed when the front door suddenly opened before they reached the porch.

"Oh," Selena said, coming out. "I was just leaving. You're back already?"

"We're both pretty tired," Cameron said. "Did the auction numbers come in strong?"

"Jerry's double checking everything, but it looks like we raised almost one-hundred thousand on the auction alone," Selena said.

"Wow, that's great," Cameron said.

Selena's gaze turned to Jane. "Do you need help getting out of that dress before I leave?"

"If you don't mind," Jane said.

And just like that, the evening with Cameron was over. He set the basket in the front foyer, and moments later he was gone. Jane went upstairs with Selena, who chattered on and on about the success of the night, while Jane only half-listened. Her thoughts were with the man she'd laughed with and danced with and who'd spent more on a basket than she made in a week.

Then she remembered, she'd forgotten to give him one of the flavored honey jars. A plan started to form in her mind of how she might take one to him and see him again, but she immediately squelched the idea.

She'd leave the jar here with a note to his mom explaining it.

That would be the rational thing to do.

"How much should I leave Mrs. Vance for the dry-cleaning bill?" Jane said as she unclasped the pearl necklace and set it in the velvet jewelry box on the vanity table.

"Oh, you shouldn't worry about it," Selena said.

Jane turned to face the woman. "I wore the dress, and I'm sure it needs to be cleaned, although I was very careful with it."

Still, Selena waved her off. "Louisa wouldn't want you to. In fact, she would be offended."

"Are you sure?" Jane asked. "I can leave some money with a note. I forgot to give Cameron some of the honey from the gift basket anyway."

"You must believe me," Selena said. "Louisa loves to help people; she would never expect you to pay for dry cleaning."

"All right," Jane said, forming another plan in her mind. Maybe she could call Cameron and discuss the dry-cleaning protocol with him. It could just be a simple, casual conversation. No expectations. She could thank him again for a lovely evening.

No. Cameron was Cameron, and she was Jane—the cleaning lady who just happened to be Cinderella for a night. The sight of her in the mirror, back in her regular clothes, drove that idea home.

"You've been great, Selena," Jane said. "I appreciate all your help tonight."

"Oh, you've been the one who's helped out tonight,"

Selena said with a laugh. "I'm sure Louisa and Cameron will be calling you to thank you again."

Jane's heart skipped a beat at the mention of Cameron calling her, even though she knew it wouldn't actually happen. That would be above and beyond Cameron's obligation—of which he had none toward her.

The evening had been wonderful, but it was over now. She headed down the stairs with Selena. In the foyer, Jane bent to open the clear plastic wrapping of the gift basket and fished out a raspberry-flavored honey. She set it on the small table by the entrance, then searched through her purse for her small notebook that came in handy from time to time. She ripped out a blank page and wrote a quick message to Cameron.

Selena opened the door, and Jane said, "I'll come out with you."

Jane followed her out, carrying the basket. "Thanks again for everything, Selena."

"No problem," she said. "I hope to see you soon."

Jane just smiled. She knew there was no chance. Her life had crossed with the Vances for the last time. She set the basket on the front seat of her car, then gave a final wave to Selena as she got into her own car.

On the drive to her dad's house, Jane finally had her thoughts to herself to mull over the evening. She'd probably read too much into Cameron's attentions toward her. But when she thought of dancing with him, especially that final dance when he'd pulled her closer, she knew that her rapid pulse hadn't been just circumstance. She liked Cameron Vance. A lot.

But tomorrow it would all fade away and become a hazy dream she could look back at once in a while. She only wished they'd taken a picture—so at least she could remember the dress. But it was probably a good thing they hadn't. It would be too hard to forget Cameron in his tux if she could look at a picture.

She turned into her dad's driveway. The porch light was on, but the rest of the house was dark. She was surprised he hadn't at least left the living room light on. But then again, she wasn't a teenager anymore.

She climbed out of the car and picked up the basket from the seat. The gourmet food would be delicious, and her father would be astounded at the price Cameron paid for it. She planned to thoroughly enjoy each item in the basket. She might even take pictures.

Jane used her key to unlock the front door, then quietly shut the door behind her. She set the basket on the kitchen table, then went into her room to change into her standard sleeping wear—yoga pants and a well-washed T-shirt. She grabbed an oversized sweater, then she went out into the backyard and set the old lawn chair on the small, weathered wooden deck. The deck was also littered with pine needles from a too-close pine tree that had probably been planted before the previous homeowner built the deck. She settled back on the lawn chair and pulled the sweater close.

The temperature was perfect, the night sounds soothing. She knew she wouldn't be able to sleep for a while, but she closed her eyes anyway, listening to the breeze stirring the aspens at the edge of the yard.

"Jane? Did you fall asleep out here?"

Was she dreaming about her dad's voice? She cracked an eye open and was nearly blinded by the sun shining right in her face.

Then a shape moved in front of the bright light.

Jane blinked. "Dad?" She must have fallen asleep in the lawn chair. She bolted up. "Oh, no. I'm late. What time is it?"

"It's Sunday," her dad said with a chuckle. Then he frowned. "Did you get drunk last night?"

"No." When she saw the doubt on her dad's face, she swung her feet off the lawn chair and stood up. "Honest, Dad. I sipped some wine, but it was too sweet." The truth was, she didn't entirely trust herself around Cameron, and wine would have relaxed some of her inhibitions.

Her dad chuckled.

He was in a good mood today.

"I hope you don't mind," he started, "but I had some of those wafers in the basket."

"That's fine, but did you check the sugar content?"

When her dad didn't answer, Jane sighed and moved past him and walked into the house. She fished the wafer package out of the garbage. Her stomach roiled when she saw the sugar content. "Dad? Come in here. We need to test your blood."

He came in, a sheepish expression in his brown eyes. He sat down like a five-year-old kid who was in trouble with his mom while Jane grabbed the glucose meter. She pricked his finger, then waited for the results.

When she saw the high number, she said, "What did you eat for breakfast?"

"Juice and that leftover blueberry muffin."

"I'm giving you a dose of insulin, then we're going to the clinic," Jane said. She prepared the syringe, then handed it over to her dad. One thing she'd always insisted on was that her dad give himself his own shots. It helped him take more responsibility.

Then she hurried into her room, refusing to listen to any of her dad's protests. She didn't have time to dress, so she tugged off her shirt to at least put on a bra. Then, shirt back on, she hurried to the front room. Her dad had just opened the door, his cane gripped in one hand.

"Come on," she said, looping her arm in his. He might be fine, but if his levels skyrocketed, he could pass out on her. So they walked arm and arm to her car, and she got him into the passenger seat, then shut the door.

Once she sat down, her dad said, "I feel all right. You're overreacting."

Jane started the engine. "If you start feeling faint, then it's too late. I hope I'm overreacting, but the truth is that you don't take your diabetes seriously enough." She handed him her phone, then started backing out of the driveway. "Look up the clinic hours. I'm not sure what they are on Sundays."

Her dad fiddled with the phone. "I can't get anything to work on this thing."

"Here," Jane said, holding out her hand.

He gave her the phone back, and she pulled over to a sidewalk curb. She quickly browsed the clinic name, then clicked on the listed website. "It opens at 10:00 on Sundays." It was only 8:45 a.m., so Jane took a right at the next street instead of a left. She didn't want to stress out her dad by telling him they were going to the hospital, but when she glanced over at him, he'd closed his eyes. "Dad? Are you all right?"

"I'm just nauseous from your driving."

It wasn't her driving, and when she pulled up to the ER entrance, his skin was very pale. She jumped out of the car, dashed through the sliding glass doors, and stopped at the check-in desk. "I think my dad's going into diabetic shock," she said to the woman behind the desk.

"Where is he?"

"In my car," Jane said, pointing outside. "Right there."

The woman nodded, then picked up the phone. Moments later two men had loaded her dad onto a gurney and wheeled him inside. Jane watched in disbelief as her father was wheeled past her, eyes shut, face drained of color.

Someone grasped her arm, and Jane turned to see that it was a lady in blue patterned scrubs. "Come sit down," the nurse said. "I'll get you some water. Don't worry, they'll take good care of your dad."

"How do you know?" Jane blurted. She felt the tears burn in her eyes, and she took a deep breath. "I'm sorry."

"It's okay," the nurse said. "I know you're worried. I'll go check to see what's going on, all right?"

"All right," Jane echoed, sitting numbly on the edge of a waiting room chair. No one else was in the waiting room, and all she could hear were muffled hospital sounds. She wasn't sure how long she waited—maybe five minutes, maybe twenty—before the nurse returned.

"Good news." The nurse sat next to Jane. "Your dad's going to be fine."

Jane exhaled and closed her eyes. When she opened them again, the nurse was waiting patiently, a smile on her face, her blue eyes friendly.

"Your dad's awake and talking, but the doctor wants to keep him for a few hours of observation." The nurse looked down at an iPad she carried. "What's his regular insulin dose, and when was his last one?"

Jane answered the nurse's questions, then said, "When can I see him?"

Another smile. "I'll take you back now."

Jane wanted to hug the woman. Instead, she nodded. "Great, thank you."

They walked through the waiting room, then down a corridor. The nurse led her into an exam room, where Jane's dad was in a hospital bed, hooked up to a monitor.

The color had returned to his face, but he looked more fragile than Jane liked.

She hurried to his side and grasped his hand.

"I'm sorry, Jane," her dad said. "I should have paid more attention to the sugar content."

Jane blinked back tears. "I should have hid that basket in my room."

Her dad gave a weak smile. "That might not have stopped me."

But Jane felt guilty anyway. She'd been good about keeping food temptations out of the house for the most part. She had a small candy stash in her bedroom, but her dad didn't know about it. "I'm glad you woke me up and told me what you did."

Her dad nodded, his gaze somber. "I'm going to do better, I promise."

Jane leaned down and kissed her dad's cheek. "A promise is a promise. I'm holding you to it."

"Now, go see when I can get out of here," her dad said.

"They said a few hours," Jane said.

A nurse bustled in, a different one than the one who'd led Jane in. "I need to take your vitals again, Mr. Morris."

Jane moved away from the bed.

"They're serving a hot breakfast in the cafeteria, miss," the nurse continued, looking at Jane.

"Oh, I'm not really dressed."

The nurse chuckled. "There's no fashion statement at this hospital."

"Go on, Jane," her dad said. "I'll be fine with Debbie here."

Jane realized the nurse's name tag said Debbie. She gave her dad a sharp look. Debbie was a nice-looking woman, maybe in her fifties. Her dad winked.

Jane sighed. She was hungry, and she might as well eat while her dad was being taken care of. "All right. I'll be back soon."

She followed the signs to the cafeteria, and she was just about to open the glass doors when someone said, "Jane?"

She'd know Cameron's voice anywhere. She slowly turned to see him crossing the lobby and coming toward her.

Eleven

Cameron wasn't sure if it was surprise or panic on Jane's face, or maybe both, when she turned around. He'd only caught a glimpse of her as she reached for the cafeteria door, but he instinctively knew that the woman in yoga pants and an oversized T-shirt, hair pulled into what might have once been a ponytail, was Jane. It just took him a minute to reconcile why he was seeing her at the hospital.

He scanned her appearance as he approached. She didn't look like this was a planned visit, more like she was dressed for curling up on a couch and reading a book.

"Hi, Cameron," she said, giving him a tight smile. .

His heart did a funny little twitch. He hadn't expected to see her here, and she definitely wasn't expecting to see him. Maybe she worked at the hospital too? "What are you doing here?"

She exhaled and looked away.

This made him worried. "Are you all right?" he asked, placing a hand on her shoulder.

She looked up at him, and he saw tears in her eyes. "My dad almost went into a diabetic coma this morning. I drove him here."

"Oh, wow. Is he going to be okay?"

She blinked a few times, as if to wish away her tears. "He'll be fine. I'm hoping he'll listen to me more after this."

Cameron shook his head. "I'm so sorry. I didn't know."

She shrugged. "How could you? And what brings you here? Is everyone in *your* family all right?" Her green eyes deepened with concern.

"I'm meeting my mom—we're presenting last night's results to the director," Cameron said. "She's running late."

"Oh, I hope the benefit was a success."

"Thanks, it was," Cameron said. "How long will your dad be here?"

"Just a few hours more," she said. "They're going to monitor him for a bit." She shook her head. "I should have put the basket in my room last night."

"The basket?" he asked.

"That food basket you bought at the auction," Jane said. "My dad ate some of the sugar wafers when I was still asleep. That and his breakfast sent his blood sugar sky high."

Cameron couldn't speak for a moment.

"Don't worry, it's not your fault—or really mine. My dad knows better." She wiped at her face. "I just can't let my guard down, I guess."

"Is your dad . . ." Cameron didn't know exactly how to put it. "Mentally healthy?"

Jane lifted a brow, and then a smile crept on her face. "He is. He's perfectly capable of managing his diabetes. He's just stubborn."

Cameron nodded. "Do you want me to talk to him for you?"

Jane looked like she was trying to hold back a laugh. "Uh, that would not go over well. He already has quite a few opinions about me going to the gala last night."

"Oh really? Like what?"

Her face pinked, and Cameron wanted to backtrack. He was being too pushy.

"I'm sure you can guess," Jane said, motioning toward him. "You're you, and I'm me. The same issue Crystal would have. Did she ever text you?"

"Wait, you just changed the subject like three times."

Jane grinned and folded her arms.

"Crystal did text me, and she's furious, but I don't care," he said. "Now, tell me what your dad's problem is with me."

She sighed. "He's just protective of me, that's all."

Cameron wanted to question her more, but just then someone came out of the cafeteria doors, and Jane moved to let them pass. Before Cameron could respond to her previous statement, she said, "Well, I'm going to grab something to eat, then go and sit with my dad."

"Wait," Cameron said, not ready for her to disappear on him. "My mom sent me some pictures from last night. Can I text them over to you?"

Jane blinked. "Pictures of us?"

"Yeah."

"I didn't know there were pictures."

"Well, there was an unofficial photographer who took a few of the event for a write-up in the local paper." Cameron shrugged. "But if you don't want them, that's cool."

Jane seemed to hesitate. "Okay, send them to me."

Cameron tried not to show that he was gloating over his victory. He didn't know why. It wasn't like he was going to contact Jane later or anything. She rattled off her number as Cameron created the contact. Then, before he could ask her more about her dad's strong opinions, she'd opened the door to the cafeteria, said goodbye, and gone inside.

Cameron stared after her for a moment, fighting the urge to go in after her, maybe sit with her and eat. What was wrong with him? Jane was clearly not interested, and it seemed her dad wasn't a big fan of Cameron's either. Besides, what was he thinking? He was swamped with work and personal fallout from the canceled engagement. He didn't have the time, or desire, to date anyone.

"Cameron?" his mom's voice cut through his thoughts.

He hadn't realized he was still standing by the cafeteria doors. He turned. "Great, you're here."

"Sorry I'm late," she said. "Did you let the director know?"

"Uh, not yet," Cameron said. "I was actually just talking to Jane Morris. Her dad is here, dealing with some diabetes stuff."

"Oh, really?" she said. "Is he going to be all right?"

"Jane says he is," Cameron said, walking with his mom away from the cafeteria.

"So she's here alone?" his mom pressed.

"Yeah, I guess so," he said. "Her parents are divorced, and her mom lives in another city." At least, he guessed that. He wasn't entirely sure where her mom was.

"We'll have to check in on her after our meeting," his mom said. "Make sure she's all right."

Cameron nodded. They'd reached the director's office, and he opened the door for his mom. He didn't know what he'd do if one of his parents had to go to the hospital. He didn't know if Jane had any other relatives in Pine Valley. Frankly, he didn't know much about her. It was hard to focus on the meeting, and he found himself more than once wanting to excuse himself to go find Jane.

When things finally concluded and handshakes were extended all around, Cameron couldn't leave the director's office fast enough.

"Do you want to go golfing with your dad this afternoon?" his mom asked Cameron. "I think I'm too worn out."

"Maybe," Cameron said. It might be good to get out in the sun and forget everything for a while.

She scanned his face, then said, "Let's go check on Jane. Then you should call your dad. He'd love you as a replacement. I tend to give up after about five holes."

"All right," Cameron said. But Jane was nowhere to be found. They looked in several waiting rooms, and short of asking the hospital staff if they could page her, Cameron gave up. He didn't want to bother her if she was in her dad's hospital room.

"I'll call her later," Cameron told his mom.

"You have her number?" She raised her brows as if this was significant.

"Sure," Cameron said, trying to brush off the look his mom was giving him. He leaned down to kiss her cheek. "I'll call Dad and see you later."

"Thanks, son," his mom said, then turned to walk out of the main entrance.

Cameron stood looking at the waiting room for a moment, then left the hospital himself. There was no use stalking the hallways. Jane was probably perfectly fine. Probably.

But to be sure, he sent her a text before he started up his car. *Just leaving the hospital. How's your dad doing? Do you need anything? This is Cameron, by the way.* He waited ten minutes, but there was no reply. So he started his car and slowly drove away.

By the time he pulled up to his cabin, she still hadn't replied. Cameron walked into the cabin and went out to the back deck. There, he sat in one of the outdoor chairs and pulled up the pictures his mom had sent over from the gala. Two had him and Jane in them. In one, they were in the background, and another person was the focus. In the second picture, the shot was closer. They were sitting at the table, looking at each other, and Jane was smiling at something Cameron must have said.

He gazed at the picture for a few moments, then attached both to a text and sent them to Jane. After a few more minutes waiting for Jane to reply, he went into the house and called his dad.

"Mom's passing up on the golfing today," he told his dad when he answered. "Want me for a partner?"

"Love it," his dad said. "Two o'clock at the club?"

"Sure," Cameron said, then hung up. He settled on his kitchen counter with his laptop and pulled up his emails. He responded to a few but kept checking his phone. Jane still hadn't replied.

He read through Crystal's texts from the night before where she called him a few choice names. Again relief washed over him at the fact that he wouldn't be marrying the woman. He screenshotted the texts, then deleted the strand. He didn't need it staring at him when he opened his text app.

Then a new text buzzed his phone, and he saw Jane's name pop up. He opened the text to read it: *Thanks for the pictures. I was in the billing office so sorry I didn't respond earlier. My dad will be fine. We just got home, and although he's grumpy about me getting rid of more treats around the house, he'll survive.*

Cameron smiled and wondered if it would seem too eager of him to text back right away? Or should he wait an hour or so? He started typing: *I'm glad your dad's okay. I have a pantry full of treats if you ever need to splurge.*

He hit SEND before he could overthink his response. It was completely casual, right?

If you have Oreos, I might be tempted.

I have regular and double-stuffed, he wrote back.

She sent back a smiley face with heart eyes.

Cameron re-read the text strand twice. Then he took a deep breath, and typed: *Let me know if your dad needs that talking-to.*

LOL. I will.

Cameron scrubbed a hand through his hair. Okay, so he would admit to himself that he liked Jane. More than a little. But now wasn't the time or the place to be thinking about another woman. His emotions were a mess, and Jane didn't deserve to be in the middle of whatever rebound he was apparently going through.

He refocused on going through his emails, then got ready to go golfing with his dad. Maybe some father-son time would clear his head.

Twelve

Jane laughed at the picture of Oreos that Cameron had texted over. They'd been texting on and off for the past week. It had all been friendly banter, and Cameron had asked about her dad a few times. She'd assured him that her dad was fine now, although she was pretty much a nervous wreck over playing the vigilante to her dad's diet and medication.

She made him start a food journal, and it was the first thing she checked when she came home from work. Tonight, Jane had curled up in bed with her Kindle, while her dad watched TV at full volume in the living room. Who cared that it was Friday night, and she was sitting home, again. She didn't mind. Not really. Tomorrow night, she'd take her dad to the assisted living center and get in plenty of social interaction.

Reading through the recent text strand from Cameron, Jane wondered what he was doing tonight. He'd sent the picture a couple hours ago—probably before he left to go do whatever wealthy single men did on Friday nights.

Jane groaned. She had to stop thinking of him as a "wealthy man"—it wasn't really fair to him. Besides, she was starting to feel that he was more than just a courteous guy. He was becoming her friend.

Her phone rang, and Jane flinched at the unexpected sound.

"Hi, Mom," she answered.

"Jane, where have you been?"

"I'm at home," Jane said, then backtracked. "Dad's house. Why?"

"Did you get my message?"

Jane pulled her phone from her ear. There were no missed calls or messages. "No, Mom. When did you call?"

Her mom sighed. Jane tried not to get worked up when her mom did this. She often made a big deal out of small things.

"Gina invited me to a weekend getaway, and I can't find anyone to watch Sparks."

Jane hid a groan. Sparks was her mom's fifteen-year-old dog that was mostly blind and had a permanent limp. "What about Mrs. Felt? Hasn't she fed him before?"

"We're not exactly on speaking terms," her mom said, breezing past any explanation. "Please, Jane. I've called everyone, and they all have excuses. You're my last resort. Can you please come get him before Sunday? We're flying out early in the morning."

"Did you call the Doggie Barn?"

"Ugh. You know Sparks got sick last time he went to that kennel."

"When did he ever go?" Jane asked.

Her mom didn't answer, which told Jane that the dog hadn't been to the Doggie Barn. "I'll give you gas money."

"It's not the money, Mom," she said. "I have to work

tomorrow afternoon, then take Dad to his game night after that. I'd have to leave at 6:00 a.m., drive two hours to your house, then back here. Plus, are you going to pick up Sparks at the end of the trip?"

"Yes, I'll pick him up," her mom said. "I appreciate this so much, sweetie. Thanks a million. Just text me when you're on your way so that I can get his medicine put together."

Jane opened her mouth to give her mom more suggestions just as her mom hung up. Jane stared at her phone. Then she closed her eyes and leaned back on her pillows with a groan. Her mom was the master manipulator. Whatever she wanted, she got. No matter how it might inconvenience someone else. Her mom was overbearing where her dad was nonconfrontational. Two people couldn't be more opposite.

Jane rolled over onto her side, plugged in her phone, and stared at the opposite wall. What would she do with an arthritic dog for a whole week? She didn't know how her dad would react, and Jane would have to make sure she stayed on top of the dog's medicine. Now Jane would have two things to worry about all week.

She sighed and climbed off her bed, then went to tell her dad she'd be leaving early in the morning to pick up Sparks. He just shook his head; they both knew how hard it was to argue with her mom.

The following morning, Jane's alarm went off at 5:30 a.m. She forced herself to climb out of bed, took a quick shower, then pulled her hair back into a ponytail. She dressed in ratty jeans and an old T-shirt. Sparks liked to drool and shed, so Jane didn't want to wear anything nice.

Before she left the house, she set out instructions for her dad and his breakfast. He'd be annoyed, but it made her feel better.

Jane jumped in her car and threw an old blanket in the back seat. Her mom refused to put Sparks in a dog carrier, so he'd be lounging all over Jane's upholstery if she didn't have a blanket to protect it. Yawning, she backed out of the driveway, then noticed that her gas tank was only a quarter full. If she filled it up now, she could make the round-trip without filling up again.

So Jane drove to a gas station to fill up. A silver Audi pulled into a parking place in front of the convenience store a couple of minutes later. Jane glanced over, wondering who else in Pine Valley was up so early on a Saturday, and the name VANCE on the license plate caught her attention. Cameron had an Audi. As Jane was trying to comprehend the coincidence, the driver's door opened, and Cameron climbed out.

Jane didn't know why she did it, but she ducked her head, avoiding eye contact. She probably looked worse than she had at the hospital. From the corner of her eye, she saw him go into the store. Great. She could hurry and leave before he came out.

Jane pulled out the gas nozzle, even though the tank wasn't all the way full, and jumped into her car. She turned the ignition. Instead of firing up, the engine just clicked, then went silent. Jane made sure the car was in park, then turned the ignition again. *No, no, no.* Her car couldn't die now. Her dad's old truck wouldn't make it out of town, and if she didn't get Sparks this morning, she'd have to reschedule her cleaning appointments—which would be a ripple effect on everything else.

Jane tried the ignition again. No luck. She wanted to scream. She dropped her head onto the steering wheel. She'd had the lube and oil done two weeks ago, and the car had passed state emissions last month. Wouldn't something have been found if there was anything wrong?

A knock on her window made her jump.

She looked up, her pulse racing, and saw Cameron standing there, a cup of coffee in his hand.

Because the car was off, she couldn't roll down the window, so she cracked open the door.

"Hi," she said. "You scared me."

"Sorry about that," Cameron said, looking at her with concern. "I wasn't sure if it was you. Then I saw the decal on the side of your car." He leaned down. "Are you okay?"

"Uh, yeah, I mean, no." Jane exhaled. "My car won't start."

His eyebrows shot up.

"The oil is fine, I just had it done."

"Can you pop open the hood?"

Jane pulled the lever, then climbed out of the car and joined Cameron as he bent over the front end. "Your power steering fluid is low."

"They should have checked that at my last oil change."

"You should still be able to start the car, though," Cameron said. "Hang on. The gas station might have some. I'll go check."

So Jane waited while he went inside. A few minutes later, he came out with a young man wearing a uniform shirt—probably the cashier in the gas station. "David" was embroidered on his shirt pocket. David pulled off his baseball cap and scratched at his red hair. He checked a couple of things, then said, "It's probably the starter. You'll have to tow it to a shop."

"Okay, thanks, bud," Cameron said, and the guy walked back into the gas station. "They don't have a power steering fluid that I trust."

"That you *trust*?" Jane asked. "Are you like a mechanic, or something?"

"Hardly." Cameron flashed a smile. "We can call Aaron's Mechanic Shop and get them to tow it to their place."

"Okay," Jane said. "When do they open?"

"I think the tow service is twenty-four hours, but the shop's not open on the weekends," he said. "Do you need a ride home?"

She exhaled. "I was on my way to my mom's to pick up her dog for the week. She's going on a trip. If I wasn't trying to get a dog here, I'd just find a bus. Well, I can actually take one to her house, then maybe drive her car back here since she's traveling by—"

"Jane," Cameron cut in. "I can drive you."

She opened her mouth, then shut it. "No," she said. "My mom lives two hours away, and her dog is . . . unpleasant."

He folded his arms. "It's no problem."

She stared at him. He was wearing a golf shirt and khakis. Was he going golfing somewhere?

"That's really nice of you," she said, keeping her determination strong. "I can't let you change your whole day to drive me. I'll just rearrange a few things and figure it out."

"Jane."

She swallowed.

"Let me help you," he said.

"But, you obviously have plans," Jane said. "I mean, you're getting coffee at a gas station at 6:30 on a Saturday morning."

"I was going golfing with a couple friends, but they won't miss me." Cameron stepped up to the car and closed the hood. Then he turned to face her again. "Let me drive you. We'll bring Sparky back. You won't have to change your schedule."

"Sparks," Jane said, hiding a smile.

"Sparks. Sparkly. Whoever. Besides. I like dogs."

Jane released a sigh. "Okay, but I'm paying for gas and for any snacks you might want."

Cameron chuckled. "Deal."

The tow truck arrived in about ten minutes, and Jane handed over her keys to Aaron himself. She was impressed to be helped by the owner of the shop, but she didn't miss the fact that Cameron gave him a couple of bills. More fifty-dollar bills?

When she climbed into his car, she groaned. "I forgot the blanket for Sparky."

"He needs a blanket?" Cameron said, starting his car.

"He sheds a lot and drools," she explained.

"We can grab one from your mom." Cameron steered his car out of the parking lot.

"Good idea," she said. "I must be more tired than I thought. Of course we can get one of my mom's blankets. I just hate to see anything happen to your car."

He shook his head. "Don't worry, really. The car will be fine."

Jane leaned her head back as Cameron accelerated. She didn't know much about Audis, but she could feel the power of the car as it picked up speed.

"Call Jeff Finch," Cameron said suddenly.

It took Jane a second to realize he was using voice recognition in his car. The call was answered, and a man's voice came through the speakers. "Hey, Jeff, it's Cameron. I can't make the tee time after all. Something's come up."

"Are you serious?" Jeff said. "This is the only time I have for weeks. Can you just come for nine holes?"

"No," Cameron said. "I'm driving a friend out of town. I won't be back until this afternoon."

"Friend?" Jeff asked.

"We'll catch up later," Cameron said.

"Wait," Jeff said. "Who's this *friend*? Sounds like a woman."

"You're on speaker phone, Jeff," Cameron said in a pointed voice. "And she can hear everything you say."

"I knew it!"

"Bye, Jeff," Cameron said, then pushed an icon on the dashboard screen. He glanced over at Jane. "Sorry about that."

"I wanted to hear what he was going to say next," she said, holding back a laugh.

Cameron scoffed. "Jeff needs to mind his own business."

She smiled. "Do you two hang out much?"

"Not like we used to." He shrugged. "I was engaged to a pretty high-maintenance woman, remember?"

"How could I forget?" Jane said. She didn't know if it was any of her business, but she was curious. "How is that all going?"

"Everything's finally canceled, at least on my end." He sighed. "My mom had Selena send out notices both by mail and email. Even though the official invitations hadn't gone out, I wanted everyone who knows me or my family to stop speculating."

"Good idea." The highway came out of the slopes of pine trees and opened into a wide valley. The sun had just broken over the eastern horizon, and the morning looked fresh and new. Jane pulled out her phone and took some pictures of the sunrise.

"You'll have to send me a couple of those," Cameron said.

"Sure." She texted some of the pictures to his phone. Then she settled back into the seat, wondering what was going on with the man beside her and why he was being so nice to her. She was trying hard not to like him more and more, but it was wasn't easy.

Thirteen

If Cameron had taken time to think of how he was about to meet Jane's mom, he might have second-guessed his invitation to drive Jane. Yet, he wasn't too worried about it—and why should he be? It wasn't like they were dating or anything; she wasn't his girlfriend. They were just fetching her mom's dog, and then he'd drive Jane back to Pine Valley.

Besides, Cameron hadn't even met her dad—the parent she *did* live with.

The drive had been just under two hours, and because it was Saturday, they didn't hit any California rush-hour traffic. Regardless, Cameron was surprised at how relaxed he felt around Jane. Whenever he had to drive Crystal just a short distance, it seemed they had to make multiple stops, and she was on her phone most of the time, either talking to a friend or texting.

Jane had taken some pictures on the way but had otherwise stayed off her phone.

She told him about the high school golf team she'd played on and how there were four coaches. "They just wanted to get out of teaching their last-period classes on tournament days," she said.

"Did you want to do more with golf? Like play in college?" he asked.

"No," Jane said. "Like I said, I wasn't all that good. It was just a fun thing to do. When I was a senior, my art teacher helped me apply to one of those fancy art schools. But when the acceptance letter came, my mom flipped out over the tuition."

Cameron glanced over at her. "Art? You're an artist too?"

"I could sketch a mean flower," Jane said with a self-deprecating laugh. "Nothing good enough to get me a scholarship—thus the tuition."

"Still, it sounds like you were accepted to a prestigious art school."

Jane shrugged. "It didn't matter, because in the long run, I still had to make money to support myself. When you meet my mom, you'll understand why I couldn't keep living with her, and my dad had his own life with his new wife. Art school would have put me into a lot of student debt, and then who knows if I would have even been able to make a living as an artist."

"So what led you to starting a cleaning business?" Cameron asked.

She told him about working as a receptionist at the office where her mom worked as a dental hygienist. "But when my step-mom died and I went to the funeral, I saw that my dad was in bad shape. So I decided to move. I got a job cleaning hotel rooms at the resort and picked up a few private clients that way. Eventually I had enough to quit the resort." She pointed to a street sign up ahead. "Turn right at the corner."

Cameron obeyed. Jane's mom lived on a quiet street in an older neighborhood. The yards were well kept, though, and he could tell that people took pride in their homes.

"It's been nice to have a break from my mom, to tell the truth," Jane said. "I love her, but . . . She's more stubborn than my dad, which is saying something. Just don't, uh, tell her your last name. She knows plenty about Pine Valley."

"Okay," Cameron said, raising his brows. "But what if she notices my license plates?"

Jane's eyes widened. "I forgot about those. Um, I guess we'll just deal with the possibility of her flipping out."

Before Cameron could ask her to explain more, she leaned forward, pointing to a two-story stucco house. "It's that house."

He slowed the Audi and pulled up to the curb. "Is this where you grew up?"

"Not exactly," Jane said. "My mom moves about every year. She always tried to stay in the same school district so I didn't have to keep changing schools. This house has an apartment. That's where she lives."

"She never remarried?"

Jane laughed. "She's had plenty of boyfriends, but none of them stick around long." She sobered. "Oh, there she is now. I should have guessed she'd be watching for me."

Cameron looked past Jane to see a woman coming up out of the stairwell stairs at the side of the house, a vision in yellow. Her yellow sundress and yellow sandals were emphasized by a yellow headband and dangly red-and-yellow earrings. Her red lipstick completed her ensemble. The only thing in common that Cameron could see about Jane and her mom was their dark hair color.

"Oh boy," Jane said, opening her door and climbing out.

Cameron did the same, and by the time he reached the sidewalk, Jane was hugging her mom.

"What's this?" her mom said, pulling away and eyeing the car. "The cleaning business must pay well."

Jane flushed. "Mom, this is my friend Cameron, and he drove me here because my car wouldn't start."

Her mom glanced at Cameron. Then her dark eyes flashed to Jane. "I told you your car is junk. Tell your father to cough up some of his money and get you something decent."

"I'm twenty-seven," Jane said. "Dad doesn't owe me a car."

"You're taking care of *him*," her mom said, still basically ignoring Cameron.

"I'm saving money on rent," Jane said.

Her mom's eyes narrowed. "You are spoiling him. When you spoil a man, he treats you like dirt." Her gaze cut to Cameron. "At least this one dresses nice."

"Mom," Jane said. "He can hear you."

Cameron took it upon himself to step forward and extend his hand. "Nice to meet you, Mrs. . . ."

She looked at his hand, then back up at him. "Morris. I still go by Morris so people don't think Jane's my stepdaughter or something." She shook his hand slowly while she looked him over from head to toe. "What line of work are you in? It must pay well if you can afford to drive a nice car. Or do you have it on lease?"

Cameron had been around bold people before, including Crystal, but Mrs. Morris might be at the top of the list. He didn't know whether to laugh or take offense.

"Mom," Jane said. "It's not polite to ask people about their incomes."

Her mom placed her hands on her hips, and yep, she had yellow nails too. "Fine. Whatever. Just make sure he takes you places that are nice, none of those fast-food joints. Make Audi Man treat you right."

"His name is Cameron," Jane said, her face reddening. "We have to get going. Is Sparks ready?"

Her mom's expression softened. "I'm going to miss him so much."

Jane grasped her mom's arm and started to tug her toward the house. Jane shot a look back at Cameron that said he didn't have to come inside. So Cameron waited outside, leaning against his car. Less than five minutes later, Jane was coming outside again, carrying a dog that looked like he could easily tip Jane over.

Over her shoulder was a bag, and behind her, her mom was bringing out another bag and a blanket.

Cameron hurried to open his trunk.

Jane's mom sidled up to him and handed him the bag and blanket. "How old are you, *Cameron?*" she asked, emphasizing his name as if it was hard to pronounce.

He shouldn't have been surprised at the question, especially after the other things she'd said to him. "Thirty, ma'am."

"Oh, he called me *ma'am*, Jane. Did you hear that?"

Jane shook her head. "Can you spread the blanket across the back seat?"

Her mom promptly handed Cameron the blanket, so he walked around the car and spread the blanket across the back seat. Sparks looked at him as Jane settled the dog into place.

"Stay, boy," Jane said. When Sparks obeyed, she continued, "Good boy. Here's a treat, but you've got to stay until I say so, okay?"

Sparks happily ate a piece of what looked like beef jerky.

Cameron moved to close the trunk of his car and turned to see Jane's mom standing with her hands on her hips again.

"You drive safe, you hear me?" she said. "I don't want anything to happen to Sparks."

Or your daughter? Cameron almost added but thought better of it. "Will do. Jane can let you know when we get to Pine Valley."

Her gaze moved to Jane's. "Did you hear him? He said you need to call me when you get to Pine Valley with Sparks."

"I will, Mom," Jane said, giving her mom a quick hug. Then she climbed into the car, so Cameron did as well.

He started the car and glanced back at Sparks. The old dog had put his head down, as if he'd already resigned himself to his fate for the next two hours of driving. Jane's mom continued to watch them as they drove away, standing like a yellow sentinel on the sidewalk.

"Sorry about my mom," Jane said. "She has no filter."

Cameron laughed. "I think you handle it pretty well."

As they got back on the interstate, Jane's phone rang. Even though Cameron could only hear Jane's side of the conversation, he guessed immediately that it was her mom.

"Hi, did we forget something?"

"Um, yes . . . that's his last name." She paused. "A lot of people have vanity plates."

Jane held the phone away from her ear for a moment. Then she said, "I don't think so. We're friends, that's all." Another pause. "Yeah, well, you can't believe everything you read on the internet."

"I'm going to hang up now," she continued. "Have a nice trip, and I'll keep you updated on Sparks." She hung up, although it was clear her mom wasn't finished talking.

Jane sighed and leaned her head back on the headrest.

Cameron glanced over at her to see that she'd closed her eyes. "Is everything okay?"

Her eyes popped open. "My mom and dad are complete

opposites, even when they never talk. My dad tells me to stay away from the Vance family, and my mom is practically demanding that you declare your undying devotion to me and propose as soon as possible."

"Undying, huh?" Cameron chuckled. "Should I take that as a compliment?"

"Not really," she said with a laugh. "My mom is always very interested in men who are successful financially. It was probably one of the reasons she and my dad didn't work out. He was an assistant manager at a discount store. Ironically, being a single mom just made her bills that much harder to pay."

"She definitely seems to live life to the fullest," Cameron said. "I've never seen so much yellow on one person, unless you count a sports fan on game day."

"You should see her when she dresses up," she said.

"Ha. I can't wait. Maybe we should invite her to the next benefit in Pine Valley." He cast a sideways look to gauge Jane's reaction. He was mostly kidding, but he wouldn't mind spending more time with Jane.

"She'd absolutely die of excitement." She shook her head. "I don't think I could handle it though. Her flirting with all of your friends would reach epic proportions."

"*My* friends?" he said. "Do you mean my dad's friends?"

"She's not picky on age."

"Ah," Cameron said. "I think I understand why you moved out."

Jane's phone rang again. "Great. It's her again."

"You can take it, I don't mind," he said with a laugh.

Jane rolled her eyes and answered. "Yes, I wrote down the medication schedule, remember?" She paused and glanced at Cameron. "No, I won't ask him that. Shouldn't you be packing?"

When she hung up, Jane turned off her phone.

"I could pull over and propose now if you want," Cameron teased.

"You wouldn't even have to pull over," she said. "Apparently my mom has been Googling you since she saw the license plate. She just informed me that a December wedding would be perfect in Pine Valley."

"Should we give her my mom's number and they can start planning?"

Jane groaned. "I'm sure your mom would love that too."

Cameron shrugged. "I was actually surprised my mom wasn't all that disappointed when I told her things were off with Crystal. She's been dropping hints about grandkids for years."

Jane met his gaze briefly. "She didn't want little Crystals running around, I guess."

He chuckled. "I think you have that right." Would his mom want little Janes running around? He dismissed that idea as soon as it popped into his head. But it was really hard to ignore the real Jane who was sitting next to him as they drove back to Pine Valley. He was finding fewer reasons to stay away from her.

Fourteen

"So . . ." Jane started, looking over at Cameron as he pulled into the driveway of her dad's house. She didn't know how he did it—staying calm and cool when Sparks had been alternating between barking and howling for the last twenty minutes of the drive despite Jane's threats of *no more treats. Ever.* "I know you're tired of my apologizing."

Cameron opened his door without a word and climbed out. Not that they could have much of a conversation over the disgruntled dog. They'd stopped at one point to see if he needed to use the bathroom, but he'd refused to get out of the Audi.

Jane climbed out too and opened the back door while Cameron fetched the bags out of the trunk of his car.

"Come on, Sparks," she said, grasping at his collar. "We're home now, or at least what will be your home for a week."

The dog growled at her. Actually growled.

"Here," Cameron said, coming up to her where she was leaning into the car. "I'll get him. Do you want him in the house or the backyard?"

Jane made the decision quick. "The backyard. His stomach is probably upset." She stepped aside and marveled as Cameron gently pulled Sparks across the seat and picked him up as if he weighed little more than a stuffed animal.

"Lead the way," Cameron said.

Jane hurried to the gate and opened it, and Cameron walked past her. He continued along the side yard, still carrying the dog. When he reached the back deck, the one that needed a good sanding, he set Sparks down.

The dog didn't move for a moment, and Jane could swear he was pouting. Then a bird flew from one tree to another at the edge of the yard, and Sparks' ears perked up. Cameron brushed his hands off. "We should get him some water."

"Well, well," another voice cut in.

Jane looked up to see her dad coming out of the sliding glass doorway, leaning heavily on his cane. She wanted to cringe when she saw that he was still in his flannel pajama pants and stretched-out T-shirt. Of course, she didn't look too much better in her old clothes either.

"Hi, Dad," Jane said. "This is Cameron Vance."

Her dad earned many more points than her mom, because he stepped toward Cameron and extended his hand. The two men shook hands, but Jane didn't miss her dad's intense scrutiny. What was it with her family?

"Nice to meet you, Mr. Morris," Cameron said.

Her dad simply nodded and turned to Jane. "I got your note, and I'll have you know that I didn't need a reminder of what to eat for breakfast."

Jane wanted to disappear. She was used to her dad like this, but it was probably a shock to Cameron.

"Okay, good to know," Jane told her dad. Hopefully, he'd go back into the house, and she could send Cameron on his way before her dad doled out any more reprimands.

"Also, tonight is Pete's birthday, and I'll be having cake," her dad continued. "If you need to alert the paramedics, then do so, but I'm eating some cake."

"That's fine," Jane said, her face burning. "You'll just have to check your levels before and after."

Her dad flexed his jaw, which usually meant he didn't want to be reminded that he needed to check his blood sugar at the assisted living center.

"Mr. Morris," Cameron suddenly said, "Jane tells me you're a great card player and keep everyone at the center on their toes on Saturday nights."

Her dad's attention was finally diverted. He *almost* smiled at Cameron. Jane wanted to hug Cameron for being so courteous.

"Are you a card player, Mr. Vance?"

"I've played a little," Cameron said. "But only for fun, of course."

Her dad eyed Cameron as if he was trying to gauge the truthfulness of the statement. "Maybe you should come tonight, then. Show us your stuff."

Jane stared at her dad. The last place Cameron would want to be was at some old folks' home, betting with wrapped candy.

But Cameron surprised her—one hundred percent surprised her. "Sure, what time?"

Jane was about to protest the invitation, to tell her dad that he couldn't expect Cameron to take out that sort of time from his schedule. But her dad had already answered.

"Seven is when things really get going," her dad said.

Jane noticed that his eyes were actually gleaming, as if he

was looking forward to this. *Oh no.* Her dad was going to use this as some sort of ego competition.

"Cameron, you really don't have to," she said, turning to him.

He just shrugged with a smile. "It might be fun. I'd like to brush up on my skills."

Jane wanted to groan. She wanted a re-do on this entire day, starting with her lame car that wouldn't start. Sparks chose that moment to rise on his creaky limbs and hobble down the deck steps, then do his business in the corner of the yard.

Maybe if Jane went back to bed, she'd wake up later to a brand-new day. But she had houses to clean, and she needed her dad's truck to do it. So she told her dad that her car had been towed to the shop, and she needed to use his truck.

"How much is that going to cost?" her dad asked.

"I don't know," Jane said. "I'll find out Monday what's wrong with it."

"Just be home before 5:00 so we're not late for the center," her dad said. "I know how long it takes you to get ready."

"I will," Jane said. Game night wasn't until 6:00, but her dad liked to know that they weren't going to be a minute late.

She walked with Cameron back around the house to his car. "Look," she said when they were out of her dad's earshot, "you really don't have to come tonight. I can tell my dad that you're busy."

Cameron stopped by his car and folded his arms. Jane tried not to notice the nice definition of his forearms.

"I won't come if you don't want me to," he said.

Jane puffed out a breath. "It's not that. You've done so much for me today, and my parents weren't exactly polite to you."

118

Cameron's mouth slanted into a half-smile. "They don't bother me. Besides, I like hanging out with you, Jane." He touched her arm and let his fingers slide toward her wrist.

His touch was light, but it seemed to vibrate through her body.

Jane swallowed against her suddenly dry throat. "I—I just didn't think you'd want to spend your Saturday night at an assisted living center."

Cameron leaned down, just a little, and said in a quiet voice, "I might surprise you one of these days, Jane." Then he straightened, and before Jane could collect her wits, he jumped into his car.

She wrapped her arms about her torso as she watched his car drive away and the VANCE on the license plate grow smaller and smaller. What was going on? And what was she getting herself into? Cameron Vance had just crossed the line from friendship to flirting, and Jane didn't know if her heart could take it.

What did he see in *her*? He'd gone through a monumental breakup, and she'd been his date to the benefit. She could admit that the red dress had made her look great that night . . . but that wasn't the real her. She looked down at her ratty jeans. Even though she'd change into black slacks and a white button down to go to her cleaning appointments, she was not the type of woman someone like Cameron Vance would date. Not that she'd admit to checking out a bunch of his pictures on his Instagram profile. Even before Crystal, the pictures made it clear that he was not in the habit of hanging out with cleaning ladies.

Jane couldn't get her hopes up, because she realized that she really liked Cameron. He was right. He'd surprised her.

She went into the house to change. From her bedroom window, she saw her dad sitting on one of the old lawn chairs, tossing a stick to Sparks. She laughed as the dog lumbered after it. Sparks wasn't as agile as he used to be, but Jane was impressed he was making the effort.

When she was ready for work, she told her dad goodbye, then went to start up his truck. She only had two houses today, but one of the clients needed almost her entire house cleaned. Apparently Mrs. Brown had had a big family BBQ the night before.

By the time Jane returned home, it was nearly 5:00, and she was in sore need of a shower. She found her dad and Sparks crashed out on the sofa together. Jane smiled and let them both sleep while she jumped in the shower. She'd fully expected Cameron to cancel on game night, but so far he hadn't sent any texts.

Jane chose a blue sundress instead of her usual Saturday-casual look. As she dressed, she wondered what she could do to thank Cameron for driving her to her mom's and back. He refused gas money, and she didn't want to overstep the bounds of their friendship. If she had her own place, she might offer to cook him a meal, but that wasn't going to happen with her dad and Sparks around. And going to a restaurant sounded so . . . official and formal. Like a real date.

Jane twisted her hair up into a messy bun. It wasn't nearly as nice as Selena had created on the night of the benefit, but it would emphasize her dangly silver earrings.

She went to wake up her dad and give Sparks his medicine.

"Looks like you two are getting along," Jane told her dad.

Her dad shrugged. "Did you get some candy for the card game?"

"I did," Jane said. "Sugar free, of course."

"I wouldn't expect anything less." He rose from the couch, and Jane watched to make sure he was okay with using his cane. Sometimes when he'd been sitting or lying down for a while, he had to take things slowly.

They left the house and climbed into the truck. Her dad insisted on driving. Jane would insist on driving home when it was dark. Her dad's night vision wasn't great, no matter how much he denied it.

"That Cameron kid isn't as snobby as I thought he'd be," her dad said.

Jane was glad Cameron wasn't with them to hear her dad. But then again, she'd been surprised by Cameron too. "He's a generous guy," she said. In truth, she was feeling pretty nervous. If Cameron did show up tonight, then how was she supposed to react to that? Surely he had other obligations, or people to spend time with.

As soon as they walked into the center, Jane heard her name called.

"Jane," Pete said, waving from his regular table. He wore his usual red-and-white flannel shirt—the one he called his "lucky shirt." "Are you staying this time?"

She smiled. "I am staying. Happy Birthday, Pete!"

"Her boyfriend is coming too," her dad said.

"What?" Pete said. "I don't think I heard you right."

"I don't have a boyfriend," Jane said, grasping Pete's hand and squeezing it affectionately.

"That's good news," Pete said with a wink. "It means that I'm still your number one."

Jane laughed.

"Oh, Jane," a woman called out.

Jane looked up to see Beatrice, or Bea, as she insisted being called. Bea had her hair colored on a monthly basis, and no matter how blonde she tried to make it, the silver strands always peeked through.

"The center brought in those sketch pads you told us to get and those special pencils." Bea held up a large sketch pad as if to prove her point.

Jane crossed over to her and looked over the art supplies. They weren't the highest quality, but they were decent. Three other women joined them at the table, and Bea brought over a bowl of fruit and a small flower vase. The other tables started to slowly fill, and games started up, everything from card games to Scrabble and Uno.

Jane found herself faced with a group of bright-eyed elderly women who were eager to use the new art supplies. So she began instructing them on sketching lines and shapes, using the fruit bowl and flower vase as examples. "You don't have to draw the bowl," she told the women. "You can draw something across the room, something from your memory, or even your neighbor."

The women chuckled at this, and Bea declared, "I'll draw you, Jane. You're looking all gussied up tonight."

Jane just smiled. "Sounds great to me." She looked about the room for her own inspiration. It had been a while since she'd drawn anything. In high school, she'd liked to fracture her drawings and combine two unexpected objects. Like a new mother cradling a world globe instead of an infant to represent how the woman held the future of the world in her arms. Or a kid peddling on a tricycle made of knives to signify that tricycles could be dangerous.

She turned back to the women at the table. Their brows were furrowed in concentration as they drew. It appeared that Bea had given up on sketching Jane and had resorted to the bowl of fruit. The elderly women were so focused and intent on their art that Jane took out her phone and snapped a picture of them. She decided to sketch the women, and later she'd add a brilliant sunset in the background to demonstrate that they were in the latter parts of their lives.

Jane became lost in her sketching as she drew the details of each woman; she'd forgotten how absorbing art could be. It wasn't until she heard her dad call out, "Well, look who showed up," that she was pulled from her concentration.

Her pulse started to hammer before she even turned to see that, indeed, Cameron Vance had come to game night. He crossed to the card table where her dad and Pete sat. Watching him from across the room was doing strange things to Jane's pulse. He wore a faded-blue T-shirt and jeans that looked as if they'd been custom made for his body. She really had to stop staring.

Just then, he lifted his gaze and saw Jane. He immediately smiled, and Jane's breath left her.

"Oh, my goodness, dear," Bea said, looking over at Cameron. "That's your boyfriend?"

"I don't have a boyfriend," Jane said, but no one seemed to believe her.

And Cameron was walking toward her table.

She swallowed and put a smile on her face.

"Hello, there," Cameron said, smiling at everyone at the table.

Four pairs of starry eyes peered up at him.

"This is Cameron Vance," Jane said, her voice sounding far away for some reason. "And this is Beatrice, Angie, Violet, and Eliza."

"Nice to meet all of you young ladies," Cameron said.

The women giggled . . . giggled! Jane felt like giggling herself.

"Is this seat saved?" Cameron asked Jane, pointing to the empty chair next to her.

"No," she said. "Do you want to draw with us?"

"How about I just watch?" he said, taking the seat next to her.

She could feel his gaze on her, and she suddenly felt very exposed. Why had she chosen to wear a sundress? Was dressing up more than usual too obvious? Jane let out a slow breath. She was in deep trouble.

Fifteen

Jane was a good artist. Really good, Cameron decided as he watched her sketching the women sitting at the table. Her hand seemed to move effortlessly, holding a dark charcoal pencil, and the lines and shapes on the pad of paper seemed to appear by magic.

He didn't know if asking her questions would make her mess up, so he remained quiet. Until the yellow-haired woman named Bea started asking him questions. One after the other. He did his best to answer, but it seemed the woman was intent on dragging out every childhood incident from him.

Finally, Jane set down her pencil and said, "Do you want to get some punch?"

"Love to," Cameron said, moving back his chair and standing.

Jane rose too, which he was glad for. He'd come tonight to answer Mr. Morris's challenge, yes, but to see Jane as well.

It seemed he couldn't see enough of her, and if he hadn't come tonight, he'd just be thinking of her.

They walked together to a table against the wall that had a couple of pitchers of punch and a plate of cookies set out. He couldn't help stealing glances at Jane. She looked pretty tonight. Well, she always looked pretty, but tonight she was wearing a sundress that flattered her. And there was a certain glow about her. Maybe it was because she was in her element of art again?

"Can we eat these if we don't live here?" he asked when they reached the refreshment table.

"Sure," Jane said. "There are several visitors here for game night, and the food is for everyone. I just thought you might want a break from my twenty-questions friend."

Cameron chuckled. "How did you know?"

Jane gave him a mischievous smile. "You were tapping your foot quite rapidly."

He lifted a brow. "You noticed that?"

Jane leaned over, nearly touching him as she grabbed a napkin, then handed it to him. "I noticed."

Cameron couldn't help following her movement and noticing how the curve of her neck led to her shoulder and the thin strap that held up her dress. For a moment their gazes locked. And he noticed how her thick lashes framed her inquisitive green eyes.

"You're a great artist," he said. "What types of art do you do?"

She shrugged. "Sketching and watercolor. But I haven't done anything serious since high school."

"Because of that whole tuition thing?"

"Yeah. That, and life."

"You should take it up again."

"You're leaning," Jane whispered.

"I am?" Cameron said, not moving from where he was apparently leaning toward her.

"Pete's watching us," she said, without breaking eye contact with him.

"Pete?"

"My dad's friend who thinks he's going to live until I'm old enough to move in here."

"Ah," Cameron said, grinning. "The guy with the red flannel shirt? He was giving me a serious once over when I talked to your dad."

"That's him," Jane said.

"Hmm." Cameron inhaled. Yep. She still smelled like summer blossoms. "I told your dad I'd play with him. Do you want to come?"

Her smile was regretful. "I'd better not. I seem to be the expert artist in the room, and duty calls."

"Okay." He knew his gaze was lingering . . . although he was no longer leaning. It was just that, even with spending four hours in the car with her, he still wanted to be with her. That was saying something, right?

She snatched a cookie and walked back to the art table.

Cameron poured a couple of cups of punch and carried them back to the card table. "Anyone want a drink?" he asked the men.

Mr. Morris looked up from his cards. "My daughter will kill me if I drink that punch. I'll have water."

"Great," Cameron said, looking about the table. "What does everyone else want?" For the next couple of minutes, he filled drink choices. Then he took a seat next to Mr. Morris.

On the next hand of cards, he was dealt into the game. A few minutes into the game, Cameron had to admit that these men were keeping him on his toes. Pete and Mr. Morris were good players, and it was only by sheer luck that Cameron won the first round. He collected his butter mints and began to play the next game.

Someone started singing "Happy Birthday." Cameron turned to see a staff member carrying a cake with a dozen or so burning candles. The staff member brought it to the card table and set it in front of Pete. Cameron joined in with the singing. He caught sight of Jane at her art table. She smiled at him, and Cameron had the urge to go sit by her again.

But he stayed in his seat as Pete clapped his hands along with the melody of his birthday song. When the song ended, Pete leaned forward and blew out the candles, in about three breaths. He sat back, triumphant, and everyone in the room laughed and clapped. Cameron included.

The staff whisked away the cake, and moments later everyone was served a slice of cake on a paper plate.

Mr. Morris frowned when his size was about half of everyone else's. "Jane must have told the staff I could only have a little."

"I'd give you mine, but it's my birthday," Pete piped up.

Cameron caught Jane looking over at her father, as if she was about to come over and make sure he didn't eat more cake than he was supposed to. Cameron hid a smile. As soon as the cake was eaten, the card game resumed.

He didn't know how much time had passed before a couple of staff members came to break up the evening.

"Ten o'clock, time to call it a night," one stern-looking woman said, hovering next to Pete.

Pete looked up at the woman. "Ah, Sylvia, won't you let us play until 10:30? Please?"

She gave him a smile but said, "We've already made an exception for 10:00 on Saturdays, and you know it, Pete."

Pete moaned but set his cards down and gathered his winnings for the night, which included butterscotch candy, a package of Jelly Bellies, and a can of Sprite that had been in big demand over the evening.

Cameron stood to shake each of the men's hands and then came to Mr. Morris. He helped the man stand and gave him his cane.

"Thank you, Mr. Vance," he said.

"You can call me Cameron, sir," Cameron said.

Mr. Morris's gaze connected with Cameron's, and the silence stretched between them. Had Cameron been too presumptuous? Rude?

"Call me Bill," Mr. Morris finally said.

"Great," Cameron said. This was a step in the right direction, right? Whatever step that was . . . he wasn't sure, but he did know that he wanted to be on good terms with Jane's dad.

The residents were hugging and kissing their friends and relatives goodbye, and Cameron walked with Bill Morris to the front doors, keeping an eye out for Jane. She was talking to a few of the ladies. Then she headed their way.

"How was it?" Jane asked, catching up with them.

"Your boyfriend's a good player," her dad said.

Jane's face reddened. "Dad—"

"Don't worry, he didn't clean us all the way out," her dad continued. "Pete was on top tonight, but next week I plan to have my A game again. Cameron is welcome to come back if he can take the heat."

"Oh, I can take the heat," Cameron said with a laugh. They followed a few people out of the front doors into the warm summer night.

He'd parked next to Bill's truck, and as they approached the two vehicles, Bill said, "How long have you had your Audi?"

"About a year," Cameron said. "I drove my first car into the ground, and my dad had an Audi for a long time. So maybe it was a nostalgic purchase."

Bill grunted. And suddenly Cameron had an idea.

"Would you like to take it for a spin, Bill?"

Jane cut a glance to Cameron. *Bill?* she mouthed.

Cameron just smiled.

"I, uh, I'm not too steady with night driving," Bill said.

"How about I drive you home, then?" Cameron offered. "You can get a feel for the car, and then maybe you can try it out sometime during daylight hours."

When Bill said, "All right," Cameron exhaled. He hadn't realized he was holding his breath.

Cameron felt Jane's incredulous gaze on him, but he acted as if it was the most normal thing in the world. He opened the passenger door for Bill, and once the man was settled, Cameron put the cane in the back seat. He shut the door, then looked across the hood where Jane was standing, staring at him.

"Meet you back at your place?" he said.

Jane only nodded.

"We might take a detour or two," Cameron continued.

She opened her mouth but then closed it. Cameron climbed into his car and started it.

He made sure Jane had started up the truck fine before he pulled out of the parking lot.

"Have you always driven a truck, Bill?" Cameron asked as he turned onto a boulevard.

"When I was a kid, my parents had a Volkswagen bus they'd let me borrow for things like high school dances," Bill said.

His tone had warmed up, Cameron noticed. Something had happened over the course of the evening that had enabled

Bill Morris to relax around Cameron, and he was glad for whatever it was.

"I've seen some of those around—rebuilt and tricked out, of course," Cameron said.

"I bought my truck brand new and paid it off in two years," Bill said, glancing at him. "You could probably pay cash on the showroom floor."

Cameron tried not to be offended. He was getting used to the bluntness of Bill Morris. "My dad worked hard his whole life to build up his manufacturing business. When I decided to go into business in college, he was pleased, but he always told me I'd still have to work for what I got. He wasn't going to just hand me a job. Turns out, when I graduated, he did hand me a job."

Bill raised his brows as if he knew this was coming.

But there was a twist. "My dad hired me as a full-time janitor."

Bill chuckled, and Cameron found himself smiling.

"So you see, it was a bit of a Catch 22 working for my dad," Cameron continued. "It was like I had to prove myself more than anyone else. But I stuck with it, and about eighteen months ago he made me the operations manager of two locations."

"Good for you," Bill said, surprising Cameron. "It sounds like you have a fine father."

Cameron couldn't agree more. "Thank you, sir."

"I'll tell you one thing, then you need to show me what this car can really do," Bill said. "Where my daughter is concerned, I don't take men coming around lightly. I'll always be keeping an eye on things. Do you understand?"

"I understand." Cameron pulled off the boulevard and drove about a mile until he came to a road that ran along a stretch of the old, deserted highway. "Ready?"

"Yep," Bill said, gripping the armrest.

Cameron stepped on the accelerator and opened up the Audi.

Bill let out a whoop, and Cameron laughed. They dragged the stretch of road several times before Bill said, "Jane's going to be upset if I'm not home soon."

Cameron just nodded. "She's probably the most responsible woman I know, besides my mom."

"I told her I already had a wife, two actually, but nothing will stop her from henpecking me," Bill said in an amused tone that clearly said he loved his daughter. "You know she's been different since she started seeing you."

Cameron didn't correct Bill in the fact that he and Jane weren't really *seeing* each other. "How so?" he asked, realizing he was very interested in this turn of the conversation.

"She's been smiling more. Laughing more," Bill said. "She's been more patient with me."

Cameron tamped down his own smile and tried not to let his ego grow too much.

"I told her not to move to Pine Valley for me," Bill continued. "But she's a stubborn woman and got it into her head that I needed to be watched over. I've been worried that she wouldn't be happy or feel like she belongs here. But it seems she's finally settling in."

They drove back to Bill's neighborhood, talking about how he used to go to Jane's golf tournaments. "They weren't easy to watch, you know. Had to rent a cart just to follow her team around. Jane hated it when I showed up. Said I had to be quiet and not cheer aloud."

Cameron laughed.

When they pulled into the Morris driveway and saw Jane sitting on the front porch steps, Bill said, "What did I tell you?"

Cameron stopped the car. "You know she loves you."

Bill didn't hesitate. "I know." He opened the car door, and Cameron hurried out so he could hand the man his cane.

Jane stood up from the step she was sitting on, and her dad called out, "I feel like a teenager with my mom waiting up for me."

"Now you know how I felt," she said in a teasing tone.

Cameron walked at Bill's pace as they approached the porch. The porch light spilled its soft glow onto Jane.

"We need to check your blood sugar," Jane said, moving aside so her dad could walk up the steps.

"I'm on my way to do that now," her dad said in a grumpy tone. But he turned back and winked at Cameron. Cameron hid a grin.

Bill enjoyed his daughter fussing over him.

"Why don't you and Cameron go out and do whatever young people do," Bill continued. "I'm going to put my feet up and watch some television with Sparks."

A bark sounded from inside the house as if Sparks had been listening—which he probably was.

Jane shot Cameron a glance as her dad went inside and greeted the dog.

"What did you do to my dad?" she asked. "He's calling you *Cameron* and shooing me out of the house."

Cameron slipped his hands into his pockets and rocked back on his heels. "We just burned a little rubber."

Jane looked past him, squinting at the Audi. "What does that mean?"

Cameron raised his brows. "So, should we go get something to eat or maybe catch a film?"

She gazed at him for a moment. "Is this a date? Because that's what people will think it is if they see us. Is that what you want them to think?"

Well, she was direct. Cameron smiled. Maybe she took

after her parents a little bit. "It doesn't have to be a date if you don't want it to be. And for the record, I don't care about what people say. I think I made that clear when I took you the benefit, knowing that everyone would ask about Crystal."

Jane rubbed a hand against her neck and sighed. "All right. Just a minute. I need to make sure my dad's blood sugar level is fine, and Sparks also needs his nightly medicine."

Cameron was fighting another smile. "I'll just wait out here. It's a nice night."

Jane narrowed her eyes but didn't try to persuade him inside. He sat on the porch step while he waited. The neighborhood was quiet; apparently, everyone had settled in for the night. He thought about Jane's question, and although he had no trouble answering, he hoped that he wasn't moving too fast. He liked her, really liked her. And he didn't want to mess it up.

"Okay, I'm ready," Jane said as the door opened.

Cameron stood and turned. "Everything settled?"

"Yeah, thanks for waiting," she said. "Where are we going?"

"Are you hungry?" he asked as they walked to his car. He opened the passenger door for her.

"I'm thinking you're hungry," she said, stepping around him and turning to face him.

They were standing rather close. Cameron allowed himself to slowly breathe in her scent. "I am. That cake was good, but not really a meal."

"Agreed, but I had a cookie too," she said. "So, why don't you choose?"

Cameron didn't have to debate the options. "Have you been to Rick's BBQ?"

"My dad loves that place," Jane said.

"Oh." He paused. "Should we invite him along?"

When she didn't answer right away, Cameron worried she was going to say yes. Instead, she leaned close and said in a quiet voice, as if she thought her dad could hear their conversation from inside the house. "No. I'll bring him something home that he can eat tomorrow. Then he won't be too upset when he finds out."

"Deal."

Jane slipped into the seat, and Cameron shut her door. As he walked around the front of the car, he felt exhilarated. Nervous too. He pretty much had Bill's approval to take Jane out, and Cameron knew that her mom already approved. He didn't know exactly why it mattered to him so much, but it did. Besides, his own parents seemed to like Jane. And . . . Crystal was out of his life for good.

Things were looking up.

They arrived at the BBQ place about twenty minutes later, laughing at the things Pete had said during the card game as well as the questions Bea had drilled Cameron with.

"You were a hit," Jane said as Cameron parked the car.

He turned off the ignition, and the interior dome light came on. He looked over at Jane. Had she put on lip gloss when she'd gone into the house? "I think it was the other way around. Everyone seems to adore you."

She smiled but shook her head, making her silver earrings sway. "They're just happy for anyone to visit."

Cameron scoffed. "That's not true. I saw plenty of family and friends around, but everyone you talked to was happy to see you."

The dome light flicked off, and her silver earrings caught the light from the lamp post in the parking lot.

"I can't believe you came in the first place," Jane said. "I know you said you'd come next week, but you really don't have to."

Cameron raised a hand to touch one of her earrings. She stilled but didn't pull away. "What if I want to?" he asked.

Her voice sounded faint when she answered. "I just don't want you to feel pressured or something."

"I don't." He moved his fingers to touch the side of her neck. Her skin was warm and smooth, and he could swear the pulse in her neck was beating as fast as his own heart. "Jane, would you believe me if I told you I liked you?"

Her eyes fluttered shut for an instant. Then her gaze was on his. "Why?"

He hadn't expected this question. But he knew why. "Because you're lovely, both inside and out. Because I can be myself with you. Because you're honest, yet mysterious."

Her lips curved into a smile. And he couldn't wait anymore. He slid his hand behind her neck and drew her toward him. She didn't resist, and when her eyes shut again, he kissed her. *Cherries.* Her lip gloss was cherry flavored.

Sixteen

Sitting in Cameron's car wasn't the most comfortable place to kiss, but Jane decided he more than made up for it as his fingers caressed her neck and his mouth explored hers. She was breathless even before he started kissing her, and she wouldn't be surprised if he could hear her pounding heart.

She slid a hand up his arm, resting it on his shoulder—it felt as solid and warm as she thought it would. Even though Cameron's kisses made no secret of how he definitely liked her, she wondered if she was dreaming. But even her best dreams couldn't compare to how it felt to be in this man's arms.

As his kiss deepened, Jane lost any reservation she might have had at the beginning and tugged him closer. His other hand skittered down her arm, then settled at her waist. She wanted to press herself against him, be closer to him. Her own wanton thoughts were making her pulse race, and the way Cameron kissed her made everything else heat up.

"Jane," he whispered against her mouth. "Did I tell you that you look great in this dress?"

She smiled. "Mmm. So if I was wearing something else, I'd be at home with my dad?"

Cameron chuckled and kissed the edge of her jaw. Then his mouth scattered kisses down her neck. "No, you'd still be here. But I wouldn't be able to do this."

Jane lifted her chin as his mouth pressed against her collarbone. Her eyes closed again as his lips made their way along the top of her shoulder.

"I thought you were hungry," she said.

"I am." His mouth was on hers again, tasting, teasing.

"That's not what I meant," she said, giving him a playful shove.

He chuckled and grasped her hand. "We should go in, as much as I'd rather stay here kissing you." When she blushed, he grinned. "Unless you want to stay here."

"We should go in."

Cameron opened his door and walked over to her side before she could get out herself. He opened her door and extended his hand. When she placed her hand in his, she felt the electricity of his touch all the way to her toes. Now that he'd kissed her, she didn't expect this intense reaction. She stood, and instead of moving back to give her room, he pulled her into his arms.

Her heart thudded as he drew her close. She moved her hands up his chest, loving the feel of his warm sturdiness, then looped her arms about his neck.

Cameron rested his forehead against hers and closed his eyes. "I like kissing you, Jane," he whispered.

She smiled. "It wasn't so bad."

He lifted his head. "What?" When he saw her smiling, he

raised one of his hands and traced his thumb along her jaw. "I can do better."

She laughed. "I was kidding."

"Good." He winked, and a split second later, his mouth was on hers again.

This kiss was gentle, exploring, as if he was in no rush at all. When he pulled back, Jane was surprised to find that she was still standing. Cameron grasped her hand and brought it to his lips. "Let's go eat."

They walked toward the restaurant together, and although a cooling breeze had picked up, Jane felt none of its coolness. Did Cameron even realize that he'd just given her the best kisses of her life? She couldn't even remember the names of any of the guys she'd dated at this point. A few kisses from Cameron, and it was like no one else existed.

There wasn't a wait, but several of the tables were filled. Jane wondered if Cameron would drop her hand. This place was *very* public, and there were certainly people here who knew Cameron. But he kept her hand in his as he told the waitress they needed a table for two.

The pretty blonde waitress smiled and said, "This way. I've got an opening in the corner booth, if that's okay."

"That's perfect," he said, giving Jane's hand a small squeeze.

So they walked hand in hand past at least a dozen tables, Cameron seemingly oblivious to the few people who looked up and gazed after them. They might not know Cameron personally enough to greet him, but they certainly knew who he was.

Cameron motioned for her to slide into the booth first, and then he slid in on the other side. He didn't sit right next to her, but it was close enough so that when he draped his arm over the back of the booth, it would be obvious to anyone who looked over that they were on an intimate date.

"So . . ." Cameron said with a grin.

Which made her feel hot all over again.

"What does your dad usually get?" he asked.

"The baby back ribs and baked potato," she said. "What about you? Are you a ribs kind of guy?"

"I knew I liked your dad for some reason."

She elbowed him, and he caught her arm, then slid his hand down it and linked their fingers together. "You didn't tell me how you charmed my dad," she said.

"I told you, we burned some rubber together."

She didn't miss the mischievous glint in his eyes. "That's it? I don't believe it."

He shrugged, tracing his thumb lightly over hand. "Guys are pretty simple. Food. Cars. And—"

She put a finger to his lips. "I don't want to hear it."

He chuckled, and she lowered her hand.

"What'll you folks have to drink?" The waitress had arrived.

They ordered drinks, and Cameron added on the loaded baked potato skin appetizer.

"I haven't tried it, but it sounds good," Jane said.

"You can't come here without trying the loaded baked potato skins," he said. "I mean, I don't even think you can say you've lived until you've eaten them."

Jane smirked. "Has anyone ever told you you're dramatic?"

He looked as if he was in deep thought, then said, "No, you're the first."

"I don't believe that."

"It's true," Cameron protested. "Now tell me my other flaws."

She raised her brows. "I didn't say that being dramatic was a flaw."

"So, it's an attribute?"

"Okay." Jane laughed. "Maybe it *is* a flaw."

Cameron's phone buzzed, and he took one look at it and turned it off.

"Work?" she asked.

"No . . . Crystal." He slipped the phone into his pocket. "She's not letting some issues drop. But let's forget about her tonight."

The waitress brought the appetizer, and after one bite Jane was hooked. "My dad would love these. He's going to regret telling us to go do something."

"We can get an order to-go," Cameron said.

Of course he'd offer. "You're too generous," she told him.

"Is that another flaw?"

"Not in this case." She picked up another potato skin and bit into heaven.

"I like that you eat normal food," he said just before eating one of the potato skins.

Jane knew he was referring to Crystal and her eating habits.

By the time their food order came, Jane wasn't feeling hungry anymore. She ate a couple of ribs, then told the waitress she'd take the rest home, along with a second order of the appetizer. The restaurant was getting ready to close by the time they left, and Jane was surprised so much time had passed.

"That was good," Cameron said. "Thanks for suggesting it."

"Funny." Jane scooted out of the booth, and he grabbed her hand again. Jane decided that she liked him holding her hand, very much.

As they walked through the parking lot, he draped an arm over her shoulders. Jane leaned into him, enjoying the cocoon of warmth and comfort being so near him brought. When he opened the passenger door to let her in the car, he stole another couple of kisses.

"Okay, Romeo, I should get home," she said.

He groaned and buried his face in her neck. Goose bumps broke out across her skin. "Did I tell you I like you?"

"I think you made that pretty clear," she said with a laugh.

He drew away, looking stoic, and as if he was making a big sacrifice in releasing her. Jane settled into the seat and sighed as she waited for him to walk around the car. She hadn't dared hope this might happen, but now that it had, she had a lot of questions. It wasn't the time to ask them, but she was feeling both nervous and exhilarated at the same time. First of all, *Cameron Vance*. And he'd kissed her. A lot. But . . . Cameron Vance.

She lived in a dumpy house with her dad and cleaned houses for a living, and Cameron . . . His family was one of the most wealthy in Pine Valley.

The door opened, and he slid into his seat.

His gaze connected with hers. "What are you doing tomorrow?" he asked as he started the car.

"Sleeping in," she said. "Then I'll be playing it by ear."

He pulled out of the parking lot, then turned onto the road leading back to the main town. "Call me when you wake up."

"Okay, bossy," Jane teased.

He said nothing, but he reached for her hand.

An hour later, when Jane was just about ready to fall asleep after going through her nightly routine, plus checking on the dog, her phone buzzed with a text. She grabbed it from her nightstand. The text was from Cameron: *Goodnight, beautiful.*

A grin spread across her face, and she felt a rush of warmth flow through her entire body. She wrote back: *Goodnight, Romeo.*

She closed her eyes and let her mind drift to the events of the evening, then further back to the first interactions with Cameron. She realized now that she'd met him at maybe the worst time possible. Was he on the rebound? Before Crystal, what had his relationship track record been? Jane told herself she wouldn't worry about it tonight. She'd go to sleep with a smile and some pretty fantastic kissing memories of Cameron.

Hours later, she woke to a huge set of doggy eyes peering at her.

Sparks nudged her with his wet nose, and subsequent slobber streaked across Jane's cheek.

"Sparks," she said, wiping at her face as she sat up. "How did you get in here?" By the bright sunlight in her room, she guessed it was at least ten in the morning.

She scratched the dog's head as memories of the night before with Cameron flooded through her and filled her heart. She leaned forward and hugged Sparks, sharing some of her joy with him. Then she remembered how Cameron told her to call him when she woke up. She grabbed her phone to see if he'd sent any other text messages. There was nothing. But she re-read their most recent strand anyway.

Sparks barked, and Jane looked over at the dog. "All right. I'll get your medicine. And did Dad feed you yet?" Probably not, since Jane had told him that Sparks needed to take his medicine the same time he ate.

Jane climbed out of bed, pulled her covers straight and grabbed a thin robe to wear until she got into the shower.

She'd take care of Sparks before calling Cameron. She didn't want a hungry dog whining in the background.

Sparks followed her out of the room and down the hallway. Her dad was sitting at the kitchen table reading the newspaper. "Good morning," he said when he saw her. "I see Sparks found you."

"Did you let him into my room?" she asked.

"He was hungry." Her dad's eyes twinkled. "I see you brought me some leftovers. I'm assuming I can have them for lunch."

"Yep," Jane said. "Cameron insisted that we get you an order of the loaded baked potato skins. They're really good."

Her dad nodded. "Cameron is a thoughtful person." His lips almost twitched into a smile, and she guessed her dad was holding back. It wouldn't do to compliment a Vance *too* much.

Jane opened one of the dog food cans on the counter, and Sparks started barking. "None of that," she commanded. Sparks slouched to the ground and whined. Jane added the syringe of arthritis medication to the dog's food and mixed it in.

Sparks didn't seem to mind the altered flavor, and he ate his food, licking the large plastic bowl completely clean.

"Good boy," Jane said. "Want to go for a walk?" She'd call Cameron on her walk. That would give her a little privacy away from her dad overhearing their conversation.

Sparks barked.

She laughed. "Okay, let me get dressed."

Once she was ready, she clipped the leash on the dog's collar. She put in her earbuds when she left the house. The walk wouldn't be much exercise for her, since Sparks moved so slowly, and Jane kept to the shaded side of the street. The summer sun was already plenty hot this morning.

She pulled up Cameron's number and hit send. It rang four times, then transferred to his voice mail. Jane hung up without leaving a message. He'd see that she called and then call her back, right?

But by the time she returned home from her walk, there had been no call from Cameron. Before going into the house, she typed up a text to send him: *Slept until 10. How about you?*

She sent it, then let Sparks into the backyard. She followed him and pulled a lawn chair into the shade. Sparks was tired out and lay down next to her at the base of the chair.

Jane double-checked that her phone was on and the volume turned up. Her text had been delivered, but she couldn't tell if it had been read. Jane pulled up the Kindle app on her phone and synced to her latest page read in her current book. But she couldn't concentrate on the plot and found herself re-reading the same couple of pages.

When Jane saw that it had been more than an hour since she'd sent the text to Cameron, she groaned. Last night had been amazing, for *her*. But maybe it had been just another date to Cameron.

Seventeen

Cameron stared at the ceiling as the morning sunlight played across the room. He'd had possibly the best night of his life with Jane, only to be turned into a nightmare when he finally called Crystal back.

He'd ignored all her texts that alternated between pleading and threatening until he returned home after dropping off Jane. The final text had prompted him to call her back even though it was after midnight. When the words: *I'm pregnant,* had shown up on his phone, Cameron had felt like the world swallowed him whole.

After talking to Crystal, and telling her that, no, he didn't want to get back together, not even for a child's sake, he hung up, feeling like crap.

Despite the fact that he knew he'd never get back together with Crystal, not for any reason, this event would tie them together for the rest of their lives. He wasn't about to become a deadbeat dad, and Crystal made it clear that she expected generous child support.

Cameron was surprised he'd slept at all after receiving such devastating news. Why couldn't the woman who became pregnant with his child be someone like Jane, or even any one of his previous girlfriends? Just not Crystal.

This would affect not only his life, but his parents, and of course his very new relationship with Jane. What would she think? If she was smart, she'd cut herself off from him. Who wanted to be with someone in as big of a mess as Cameron was in?

And now, in the light of the morning, nothing seemed better. The crushing weight was still there, and Cameron's head was killing him. He'd left his phone off all night and couldn't bring himself to check what were surely texts and missed calls from Crystal. She'd already demanded that he cover her prenatal care. Which of course he'd help with, but wasn't that what insurance was for? Then she reminded him that she'd quit her job permanently when they'd started wedding plans. She hadn't had time for both. He'd responded that he'd thought she was taking a three-month leave of absence, not quitting.

No wonder his headache felt like someone was stabbing him with a knife over and over.

And, he couldn't forget that in the middle of all this mess was an innocent baby who'd be born—according to Crystal's calculations—in seven months. *February.*

Cameron groaned.

He dragged himself out of bed and into a scalding-hot shower. If only he could wash away the entire few months he'd been with Crystal. She'd told him she'd been on the pill, but her response was that all birth control was only ninety-five percent effective. Why hadn't she told him earlier? She said she'd suspected for a couple of weeks, and that her emotions had led her to "nesting," as she again tried to justify taking his credit card and spending thousands on new furniture. Cameron told her they still weren't getting back together. He'd hung up when she started screaming at him.

But as the hot water sprayed over him, he wondered. If he had known about the pregnancy earlier, would he have tried to make things work with Crystal? Would he have followed after Jane? Would he have allowed himself to kiss her last night?

Another groan.

When Cameron had dried off and dressed and gotten the first cup of coffee in him, he finally went back to his room to fetch his phone. He sat on the edge of his bed and turned his phone back on.

Three texts from Crystal. No surprise there.

A missed call from his mom. She was probably inviting him to Sunday dinner. And . . . Jane had called, then left a text.

He read through her text and felt his heart twist. He'd told her to call him when she'd woken up, and she had. His request had been so simple, so hopeful, and now . . . everything had changed. He'd have to tell Jane about Crystal, and he knew that the news would suck all the way around. Jane would be hurt. She'd go back to her life before they'd met. And he would be one of those jerks that she'd look back on and wonder what she'd been thinking.

Cameron hung his head and closed his eyes. He'd have to tell her. Today. As soon as possible. It was only fair. Besides, Jane could very well hear the news from someone else. Cameron wouldn't put it past Crystal to make sure that she did. Some of Crystal's nasty accusations against Cameron had included his playing the field with their former cleaning lady.

He picked up his phone and called Jane. He winced when she answered, her voice full of expectation. "Jane," he said. "We need to talk, in person."

"Okay," she said, the wariness plain in her voice.

"Can you come over?" he asked. "Or can we meet somewhere privately? I don't want to involve your dad in our discussion."

"Does it have something to do with my dad?" she asked, worry now in her tone.

"No, nothing like that," Cameron said. "I just . . . need to talk to you in person."

"All right." Her voice was soft, resigned. "I can leave here in about half an hour. I'll come to your place."

Cameron exhaled, but it was far from relief that he felt. "Okay."

He hung up and remained still for several moments. Then he replied to Crystal's text with: *I need to think through everything. I'll contact you tomorrow.* Cameron might have to let go of Jane, but he refused to let Crystal worm her way back in. Until the child was born, he wanted very little contact with her.

Cameron pocketed his phone and went downstairs to wait for Jane.

The thirty minutes was closer to an hour when her truck finally drove up the road to his cabin. Cameron went outside immediately and watched her climb out.

She was wearing a V-neck black shirt and slim-fitting capris with sandals. Her hair was down, framing her shoulders. The dark, troubled look in her eyes tugged at his heart and made him feel terrible. As she walked toward him, he came down the stairs to meet her. Before he could stop himself, or think of how much he was confusing her, he pulled her into his arms and buried his face in her hair. He breathed her in for a long moment, feeling her soft body against his as she held onto him.

"Cameron, what's wrong?" she asked, drawing away, even though he didn't let go. "You're scaring me."

Finally, he released her and stepped away. He scrubbed a hand through his hair. He moved back to the steps and sat down.

Jane came to sit by him. "Just tell me," she said. "My stomach is in knots."

Cameron met her steady, worried gaze. She was right. He just had to say it. "Crystal's pregnant." He looked away then. When it came to it, he didn't want to see the pain and questions in Jane's eyes.

After a long moment, she said, "I'm assuming it's your baby."

"That's what she says."

Jane went quiet again. "Are you getting back together again?"

"Hell, no," Cameron spat out. "I'll provide for the kid, of course, and I want to be a decent dad." He spread his hands. "All of this isn't fair to an innocent kid. It's not fair to you either."

He finally looked at her. She wasn't looking at him like she was disgusted. But she was hurt, and there were tears in her eyes.

"Jane, I'm really sorry," he said. "I didn't mean to make a mess of things, of *us,* but this kid is going to keep Crystal in my life forever. And I don't anticipate things getting any easier. Crystal has already been texting over demands this morning. I can hardly stand to open her texts, but I have to look beyond my own ego and feelings and think about the baby."

Jane blinked. "What are you saying, Cameron?"

He swallowed against his dry mouth. "I don't expect you to . . . stick with me. Ever since we started becoming friends,

I've been on a rollercoaster. And it's not fair to expect you to deal with my problems. You're dealing with your dad and—"

"Cameron," she cut in. "Crystal's pregnancy isn't something that would make me give up on you." She brushed her fingers along his jaw, and he wanted to lean into her, take comfort from her touch. But she wasn't finished talking yet. "I believe you when you say your relationship is over, but I also understand how things can change. You just had life-changing news, and I don't want to stand in the way of you making the decision you need to. I get that our friendship started under stressful circumstances, but life is stressful in general. I'm not saying that you're on the rebound with me, but I am saying that you have a lot of things to work out before you can consider getting into a new relationship. And maybe I do too."

The tears were back in her eyes, and Cameron felt his heart start to rip.

"You're a lovely man, Cameron Vance," she said, leaning close and kissing his cheek as her hand strayed to the other side of his face. She drew back, holding his gaze. "I like you too, and when you're ready, call me. Maybe I'll still be around." She rose to her feet and brushed off her pants. "Thank you for everything."

Cameron couldn't speak over the lump in his throat. He watched her walk back to her car and climb in. As she turned the car around and started to drive away, he rose to his feet to call after her. But she couldn't hear him, and he knew she was right. He had to figure his life out. Crystal had torn him to pieces. And now there was a baby in the mix.

Cameron pulled out his phone, wanting to call Jane. To beg her to come back. But she didn't deserve a confused man. So, instead he called his mom as he walked to the backyard. As he paced the deck, he told her everything. About how he was falling in love with Jane. About her mom. About her dad. About Sparks. Then he told his mom about Crystal and how she was having his baby in February.

His mom was silent for a long time, and Cameron wondered if the call had dropped, or if he'd shocked his mom into a heart attack.

"Son, did you not use birth control?"

Cameron exhaled. It wasn't too fun discussing this with his own mother. "She was on the pill."

His mother scoffed. "Sure she was. Or . . . have you considered the other alternative?"

"I don't think Crystal slept with another man," Cameron said. "She was practically with me twenty-four-seven."

"No, I mean that she's *not* pregnant," his mom said.

"What?"

"Think about it," she said. "Crystal is desperate to get back together. You're a great catch—sorry to be blunt—but you know that money attracts the piranhas. Crystal might use this to get back together. You marry her after all, then she'll conveniently have a miscarriage."

Cameron sat down on the edge of one of the deck chairs. "How do I find out if she's really pregnant?"

"Well, time will tell, of course, but there might be a quicker way," his mom said.

"How?" Cameron prodded.

"Tell her you want to go to her next doctor appointment with her," his mom said. "Insist on an ultrasound. And even then, when the child is born, do a paternity test."

Cameron exhaled, his mind reeling. "Do you think another human would really stoop this low? Even Crystal?"

"I don't know," she said. "But I do know you shouldn't let this come between you and Jane. If anything, you need her more than ever. If you really like her, son, you shouldn't be choosing Crystal over her."

"I'm not choosing Crystal," he said. "Things are so screwed up right now, how is that fair to Jane?"

"*Life* is messy," his mom said in a firm voice. "You're choosing Crystal over Jane if you are letting this come between you. No matter the outcome of Crystal's pregnancy, do you still choose Jane?"

Cameron closed his eyes. "Of course."

"Then choose her *now*," his mom said. "Waiting will drive a wedge between you. If you choose Jane now, before the paternity is verified, before the baby is born, then Jane will believe that your feelings are true."

"You're right," Cameron said. After he hung up with his mom, he remained on the back deck, sitting in the sun and letting it warm him through. He was going to follow his mom's advice and tell Crystal that he was coming to her doctor's appointment. He was also going to figure out how to keep Jane in his life.

Eighteen

Jane didn't know why she bothered to dress up for game night at the assisted living center. It wasn't like anyone under the age of seventy would be seeing her. This time last week she was anticipating Cameron coming. But all had changed. Last week seemed like a lifetime ago. Everything had seemed so different then, so simple.

Cameron was out of her life now; she hadn't heard from him since Monday night when she'd gone to the shop to pick up her car. The starter had been replaced, but the invoice had a zero balance. When she confronted the shop cashier, he had raised his hands, saying he wasn't sure who paid the bill but there was no balance for her to pay.

Jane had immediately thought of Cameron. She'd sent him a text even though they hadn't had any contact since their goodbye on Sunday.

He'd texted back: *Let me do this one thing for you.*

In truth, he'd done a lot more than just one thing for her. This morning as she'd loaded up Sparks in her car and driven him back to her mom's, she'd thought of the drive she'd taken with Cameron and the excitement she'd felt being around him. She wondered how he was doing with the whole revelation about Crystal being pregnant. Would they get back together after all? Having a child together would be a pretty strong bond to ignore.

She missed him. She missed his laugh, the way he looked at her, even their arguments. But she'd known from the beginning Cameron Vance was too good to be true.

Jane faced her bedroom mirror. She'd gone on a mini shopping spree on the way back from her mom's. It was probably therapy to get over the incessant questions her mom had asked about Cameron. Jane wore a new pale violet blouse with a tiny print, along with new jeans—which looked old because of the trendy rips in them. But they'd both been on clearance, so Jane was proud of her find.

"Jane?" her dad called.

She'd delayed long enough, and her dad would be driving himself if she didn't hurry. "Coming," she said.

Her dad waited by the door, and they walked out together into the cool summer evening.

"Looks like rain," her dad said.

Jane glanced up at the dark clouds hanging low in the sky. It did look like rain. Yet she didn't feel like she needed a jacket. The center was always plenty warm. "Do you want me to grab your jacket?" she asked.

"No time now," her dad said.

Jane hid a smile; her dad was so strict about being on time to game night. They climbed in her newly repaired car, and just like that she was thinking of Cameron again. She wondered how many weeks would have to pass before she didn't think about him every other minute.

"Is Cameron coming tonight?" her dad asked on the drive to the center.

She wondered if her dad was just trying to get under her skin. "I told you he's not coming. He's out of town or something." She didn't want to spell it all out for her dad—explain that Cameron's ex-fiancée was pregnant. She figured if Cameron wasn't coming around anymore, her dad would eventually stop bringing him up.

Once they arrived at the center, Jane was once again caught up with Bea and the ladies in their art group.

Bea, who wore a pink striped shirt and a pink cardigan, along with her usual silver glittery headband, waved Jane over. "We've got water colors!" she pronounced.

"Oh, great," Jane said, smiling. "You ladies are getting spoiled."

The women smiled back at her, and Jane went about setting up water cups. "We'll work off our sketches we did last week. You want to start with the darker colors first, then add bits of the lighter colors." She moved around the table, getting each lady started on her project. Then Jane settled in her own seat. She'd finished her sketch of the ladies, and tonight they were sitting in a different order. But that didn't matter when adding color and the sunset background.

She pulled up the picture she'd taken last week on the drive with Cameron. It was a sunrise, and so she decided to paint the colors of a sunrise instead. After all, these women were like a sunrise in Jane's life. Soon, she became absorbed in her work.

"Is your man coming tonight?" Bea asked, pulling Jane from her concentration.

She looked up. "Um, I don't think so."

"My eyes aren't very good anymore, honey, but isn't that him sitting by your father?" Bea continued.

Jane looked over at the card table where her dad was sitting with Pete. Her breath caught when she saw who was sitting next to her dad. Cameron was wearing a pale-green, button-down shirt, his sleeves rolled up to his forearms, and a loosened navy tie. He looked as if he'd come from a business meeting and didn't have time to change.

She knew she was staring, but she was truly shocked. There'd been no communication with him since Monday night, yet . . . he was hanging out with her *dad*? She didn't know whether to laugh about it or be annoyed.

Cameron chose that moment to look up, and their gazes met. Jane had no idea what to think. He gave her a nod of acknowledgment and went back to playing the card game.

"I guess his meetings got out early," Jane said, realizing the women at the table were watching her. She felt a slow heat creep up her neck, and she refocused on her watercolor. But the colors all seemed to blend together, and she realized she had tears in her eyes.

Oh no. She couldn't cry here, not right now. Not with Cameron sitting a few tables away. Bea would notice too. She waited as long as she dared, then said, "I'm going to the restroom. I'll be right back."

She rose and hurried away from the table. She bypassed the hallway with the public restroom and walked out the front doors. It had started to rain, but she didn't mind. She leaned against the wall, protected by the awning from the driving rain. Closing her eyes, she wondered why Cameron had come. What was he trying to prove? Surely, he and her dad hadn't bonded *that* much over burning rubber.

So, that left only one option. He'd come to talk to her. Did he feel obligated to tell her in person that he and Crystal were going to get back together after all? It was just like him to have the courtesy to tell her in person. Well, then, she'd just have to take it like the adult woman she was.

Something shifted in the air, and the sound of rain seemed to dull. Jane sensed Cameron's presence. She opened her eyes to find him walking toward her

He stopped next to her. "Jane?" he said, touching her arm, concern in his eyes.

What did he have to be concerned about?

She moved a couple of inches, and he dropped his hand. It hurt to look at his handsome face and the mouth she had kissed and the eyes she'd become so caught up in.

"I was just hot in there," Jane said. "What are you doing here?"

"I came to find you," he said, his gaze searching hers.

Why did he have to look at her like that? As if he was still interested in her?

"But you seemed so absorbed in your work, and your dad called me over to play," he said.

Jane exhaled. "You could have called instead of coming to tell me." She felt petty for saying it, but the blow wouldn't have hurt so much over the phone. And there wouldn't have been the risk of crying in front of him.

"Believe me, I've thought about calling you every minute of each day, but I just got back in town an hour ago." Cameron stepped closer. "This isn't something I wanted to say over the phone."

Jane's heart sank. After Cameron told her what he came to say, she didn't think she could go back in and face a roomful of people. Maybe she could hang out in the bathroom until her dad was finished.

Or the car. That would be better. "I don't need to hear every detail," Jane said. "I'm happy for you and Crystal. Every kid deserves a two-parent home. I understand that more than a lot of people." She pushed off the wall and headed across the parking lot toward her car.

"Jane," Cameron called after her.

But she ignored him, just as she ignored the rain pelting her face. She was almost to the car when she realized she'd left her purse and keys inside the center.

"Jane." Cameron caught up with her and wrapped a hand about her arm. "What are you talking about? Crystal and I aren't getting back together. I came to tell you I don't want to do this without you."

Jane gazed up at him in the rain. "You don't want to deal with Crystal and your kid without me?"

He exhaled and moved closer. "I don't want to do *anything* without you. Whether or not Crystal is really pregnant, it doesn't matter. I don't want it to come between us."

"What do you mean?" Jane stared at him. "She might not be pregnant?"

"My mom has her doubts, and I'm going to Crystal's next doctor appointment to find out for sure," he said in a rush. "Even if she is pregnant, I'm going to have a paternity test done when the kid is born."

"And if it's your kid?" Jane prompted, folding her arms.

"Then it's my kid, and I want shared custody," Cameron said. "But that's all." He rested his hand on her shoulder and leaned in. "You're the woman I want, Jane. Not Crystal. Not anyone else. Whether or not Crystal is having my baby, I want to be with *you.*"

Jane brushed at the tears on her cheeks that had mingled with the rain. She'd started to tremble. "Are you sure?"

"Yes," he whispered back. He moved his hands to cradle her face as he gazed into her eyes. "Jane, I want you back. It's killing me not to be with you. I was shocked, confused, but I never stopped wanting you."

Jane blew out a slow breath. Then she slid her hands up his solid chest. His shirt was damp from the rain. She raised up on her toes and pressed her mouth against his.

Cameron wrapped her in his arms and kissed her back with an intensity that made Jane feel like she was floating above the ground.

When they both got to a point where they had to catch their breaths, Jane drew away. "Wait. Does your mom know . . . about me?"

Cameron grinned. "She does. And she's thrilled."

Warmth buzzed through Jane. "Really?"

"My dad too," Cameron said. "You were the first person he asked about before our meetings started. The question is, will your parents be okay with us?"

Jane smiled. "My dad was looking forward to you coming tonight, but I told him you were out of town. And, well, you know my mom."

"Um-hm," Cameron said, placing a light kiss on her lips. "We're really wet."

Jane laughed. "I think everyone's going to be staring at us when we go back inside."

"So, let's go get hot chocolate or something," he said, sliding his hands along her arms, then linking their fingers. "I'll go tell your dad, and then we can come back here to pick him up."

Jane was tempted. She knew she'd probably kiss Cameron for the next hour if they were in his car. "I need to get back to the art table."

Cameron nodded, although he looked reluctant to agree. "Okay. Let's get you out of this rain, then." He tugged her toward the center, and she laughed as they ran to the front entrance, narrowly missing a growing puddle of water.

Jane made a detour to the public restroom where she used the blow dryer to get as dry as possible. Cameron was waiting in the hall for her when she came out.

She laughed at his appearance. His shirt was damp, and his hair was still dripping. She reached up and flicked away some of the water droplets. Cameron caught her hand and pulled her against him.

"Not here," she said, although she wanted nothing more than to kiss him again. She gave him a single kiss, then pulled away despite his groan of protest.

"I'll see you in there," she said, then went into the main room.

"Looks like you got caught in the rain," Bea said as Jane retook her seat.

Jane just smiled and continued with her watercolor. She sensed when Cameron came back into the room, but she didn't turn around to look. Her phone buzzed, and she pulled it out of her purse.

What are you doing later tonight? Cameron had texted.

Jane wrote back: *Soaking in a hot bath. My feet are freezing.*

I have a hot tub.

Jane's face warmed. *I know.*

Do you want to come over?

I probably shouldn't, she wrote, then added, *Tempting, though.* The truth was, she hadn't wrapped her mind around the fact that Cameron was here, and they were pretty much officially dating. Or at least, they'd better be.

The offer stands if you change your mind, he wrote.

She returned to her watercolor, and a few minutes later her phone buzzed again. Jane picked it up from the table.

Cameron had texted: *Do you want to come to Sunday dinner at my mom's tomorrow night? It's sort of a tradition. You can bring your dad too.*

Jane looked over at the card table. Sure enough, Cameron's eyes were on her, and as their gazes met, he winked.

Jane's heart thumped, and she looked down at the phone. *I'll let you know.*

Say yes, Jane.

She couldn't stop herself from looking over at him again. The heat from his gaze made her feel like he was sitting next to her and not across the room. So, she returned to her phone and wrote: *Yes.*

Nineteen

Cameron opened the doors before Jane could ring the doorbell to his mom's house. He'd seen her car pull into the curved driveway while he was standing in the front living room. She'd come alone, and he wasn't sure where her dad was, but he was glad to see her. She hadn't gone out with him after game night, but they'd texted late into the night. And when she called him this morning when she woke up, they'd spent another hour on the phone. Cameron had quite enjoyed her morning voice.

Tonight Jane wore a long turquoise sheath with a slit up to her thigh.

"Is your dad not coming?" he asked as he reached for her hand and kissed her cheek. He breathed in summer blossoms.

"He's expecting a visit from a cousin who is passing through town," Jane said. "I feel dumb not bringing anything."

"Believe me, my mom and Selena always go overboard," Cameron said, leading her into the house. "I'm glad you came." They walked into the living room, where his dad was sitting on the couch and flipping through a magazine.

His dad shot to his feet. "Great to see you again, Jane," he said, extending his hand.

She stepped forward to shake his hand. "I appreciate the invitation."

Mr. Vance grinned. "We're pleased that Cameron issued it. If he hadn't, I would have."

She laughed, and Cameron was more than pleased about his family's warm acceptance of Jane.

His mom bustled into the room. "Cameron, can you slice the ham? Oh, Jane, you're here. Welcome." She looked about the room. "Is your father here?"

Jane explained about her dad, then offered to help in the kitchen.

"No, dear, you can sit and relax," his mom said. "You're our guest. Besides, Cameron is the designated meat carver."

Jane raised a brow, and Cameron said, "What she means is that when I'm here for dinner, my dad gets to put his feet up. I take care of any manly duties."

"Carving meat is manly?" Jane asked, a smirk on her face.

His dad chuckled and said, "In this house it is. Carving meat and doing dishes."

Jane's mouth curved into a smile, and Cameron could see she was pleased. That made him pleased.

He felt reluctant to leave her, but he couldn't just sit and stare at her while in the same room as his dad. So he followed his mom into the kitchen and set to work on slicing the glazed ham.

"You know, Mom," Cameron started, "they sell hams pre-sliced. Saw one at the grocery store."

"Of course they do," she said. "But Selena says they dry out faster."

Selena came into the kitchen just then, carrying a pitcher of what looked like her famous strawberry lemonade. "Your mother's right," Selena said. "The juices stay inside the ham if you wait to slice it after it's baked."

"All right, all right, I believe you," Cameron said, refocusing on his task.

"We like her," his mom said in a quiet voice.

He looked over to meet her gaze. "Jane?"

His mom smiled. "Yes, *Jane*. I don't know what's going on between the two of you, but she's welcome here anytime."

Cameron straightened. "Thanks, I like her too."

Selena laughed.

"What's funny?" he asked.

"I think you more than like her, Cameron Vance," Selena said with a knowing look. She picked up a tray of glasses. "When you're finished with that, transfer it to the silver platter, then bring it outside. We're eating on the deck."

"Yes, ma'am," Cameron said and earned himself another laugh.

When Selena walked out of the kitchen, Cameron turned to his mom. She was stirring some sort of creamy pudding into a bowl of cut-up fruit.

"Am I that transparent?" he asked. "I mean, Selena hasn't even really seen us together."

"Oh, you're transparent," his mom said with a smile. "But I have no problem with that." She set the bowl aside and rinsed off the spatula in the sink.

Cameron exhaled. He was glad Jane had been willing to listen to him last night. This coming week, though, he was facing a doctor's appointment with Crystal.

"When's the appointment?" his mom asked in a soft voice. It was like she could read his mind.

"Wednesday afternoon," he said. "I guess I'll find out the due date at least."

His mom pressed her lips together in that pert way of hers. She dried off her hands and walked to the fridge. She opened the door and brought out a veggie tray she'd already put together. "Do you want me to come with you?"

"No," he said. "I don't want to involve anyone else at this point, unless I have to."

His mom nodded. "If you change your mind, let me know. I could even stay in the waiting room." She fetched a silver platter from a cupboard and set it by Cameron.

He proceeded to transfer the sliced ham onto the platter. Then he carried it through the dining room and out the back doors that led to a massive deck.

Selena and his mom had already set the table and put up the large umbrella to provide shade. The air had started to cool from the warm afternoon. His mom arrived behind him, carrying the fruit salad. Cameron went back inside to fetch more food.

He wished he hadn't started thinking about the doctor appointment with Crystal. He wasn't looking forward to seeing her again. His mind veered into the questions his mom had asked him last week. What if Crystal was faking the pregnancy to get him back? But then, why would she tell him about her doctor appointment?

He tried to shove those thoughts away as he carried out the rest of the stuff. On his final trip, Jane and his dad followed him outside. The seating arrangement wasn't pre-planned, but Cameron ended up sitting across from Jane. He was more than happy to be able to see her from this angle, but he would have rather been sitting a lot closer.

Jane gave him a sympathetic smile from across the table. *Hmm.* Maybe he *was* transparent.

Selena sat and ate with the family as well. As long as Cameron could remember, his mom had always insisted that Selena join them for meals when she was around.

Most of the conversation during dinner was about the Fall Festival his mom was helping to coordinate for Pine Valley. She was on the planning committee, and Cameron listened while Jane offered some ideas that his mom seemed to like.

He found himself loving the interaction between his mom and Jane. It was another thing to add to what he already liked about her.

At the end of dinner, Cameron rose to his feet. "Well, I'm on dishes duty. I'll just leave the rest of you to enjoy your dessert."

Jane met his gaze. "I'll come and help."

"Oh, you don't have to, Jane," his mom cut in. "You're our guest. And besides, Cameron is great at his job."

Jane smiled at his mom. "I want to help. I might be able to show him a thing or two."

"That's right," his dad said, piping in. "You do run a cleaning business. You can correct the fallacies of the Vance family."

Everyone laughed, and Cameron was more than happy to walk into the kitchen with Jane as they carried back the dishes. They made one more trip, then Cameron turned on the hot water in the sink and began to scrub the larger pans. He'd hand-dry them, then put the regular dishes into the dishwasher.

Jane joined him at the sink after putting away the salt and pepper shakers and the fancy mustard his dad liked with the ham. Having her stand side by side with him made it too tempting to kiss her. So he did, just a little one.

"Cameron, your hands are wet," Jane said.

"Sorry," he said, removing his hands from her waist.

She faced forward again and nudged him. "I didn't know you were so domestic."

"At my own home, I'm pretty lazy."

Jane laughed. "You can get on my waiting list."

Cameron set a pan on the side board to drip dry while he found a kitchen towel. "You have a waiting list?"

"Yeah, and I just put out a notice to hire someone part-time," she said as she loaded the glasses into the top rack of the dishwasher. "Mondays and Fridays are killing me. Everyone wants their house cleaned either before or after the weekend."

Cameron started to dry the pan. "You work too hard."

She glanced up at him and paused. "I don't mind the work, and I don't work harder than anyone else I know. Look at your mom. She'd the hardest-working lady I know and probably doesn't make a dime."

"True." Cameron set the dry pan on the counter, then started scrubbing the next dish. He cast Jane a sideways glance. "Have you ever thought about going back to your art?"

Jane sighed. "I'm rusty. I couldn't just start painting for galleries. My education is way behind that of the other artists out there. This industry is about connections, and I've lost touch with pretty much anyone I used to know. Plus, I'm about a month away from moving out from my dad's, and when I get back from work I can barely lift a finger. And even when I move out of my dad's place, I'm still going to have to help him a lot."

"Maybe you can do art school part-time once you get someone hired to help you," Cameron said.

"Maybe. I'd have to raise the cleaning rates, though," she said. "I don't know if my clients would go for it."

"You're worth it," Cameron said. "I've never seen a better organized dishwasher."

Jane narrowed her eyes and swatted his arm, but he laughed and pulled her against him. She wrapped her arms about his neck, seeming not to mind his wet hands any more.

He couldn't resist kissing her again.

"I thought you were doing dishes," Selena said, coming into the room.

Cameron broke away from Jane. He knew his face was heating up, but he wasn't really embarrassed. Jane just laughed and turned back to the dishwasher.

He caught sight of Selena's smile.

"You two are excused," Selena said. "I'll finish up in here."

"We've got it," Cameron said.

Selena folded her arms. "That wasn't a request."

"All right, all right," he said, reaching for a towel to dry his hands. He looked over at Jane. "Do you want to go on a walk or something?"

"I'd love to."

He grabbed her hand and led her out of the kitchen, calling, "Thank you, Selena," over his shoulder. Then he spoke to Jane. "There's a pretty cool walking trail that winds above the neighborhood here," he said as they stepped outside.

"Sounds good to me."

They walked down the driveway, then to an access path that led to the walking trail. Pines towered overhead, lining both sides of the trail and providing plenty of shade.

"This is really beautiful," Jane said. "I didn't even know this was here." She snapped a couple of pictures with her cell phone.

"My dad used to take me on walks here when I was

younger. I guess it was a good chance for those deep father-son discussions."

"You two seem to have a great relationship," she said.

"Yeah, I got lucky," Cameron said. "That's why if I'm having a kid, I want to be involved in his or her life."

"I'm glad you feel that way," Jane said.

He slowed his step and slipped his arms around her. He gazed into her eyes—eyes that were so easy for him to get lost in. "You're an amazing woman, Jane."

"I think you're pretty amazing too," she said, moving closer. "And you'll make a great father."

"Your support really means a lot," he said.

She ran her fingers along the back of his neck, then tugged him closer.

He obliged, not minding at all that Jane wanted to kiss him as much as he wanted to kiss her.

Twenty

Jane had been checking her phone off and on for an hour. Today was the day that Cameron was meeting Crystal at her doctor's appointment. Jane had tried not to let her insecurities about Cameron creep in while she waited for his phone call. Ever since that night at the assisted living center, and their kisses in the rain, everything between them had been like a fairy tale. But Jane was a realist, and she knew the rainbow bubble would pop sometime.

The doctor's appointment would be a big dose of reality, for everyone.

And Jane's heart hurt to think about it. She was more than impressed that Cameron wanted to be equally involved in his baby's life. But she also knew the bond a child created between a man and a woman was like nothing else. It was why she suspected her mother was so hurt when her dad remarried, and why her mom had never remarried herself.

Her phone buzzed in her pocket, and she turned off the vacuum she'd been using at the Daleys' house. But the text was from someone inquiring about the ad she'd posted on the Pine Valley website. She wrote back a quick reply with a possible interview time.

Jane slid her phone into her pocket and turned the vacuum back on. The work was mundane and gave her plenty of time to think about Cameron. His family was great, and even though she and they existed in different spheres of life, his mom and dad had been nothing but accepting of her. And Cameron had been great with her dad. Jane didn't worry about her own mom because her mom always ran toward dollar signs.

Jane reached the edge of the area rug and switched off the vacuum. The Daley home had mostly wood floors, but Mrs. Daley liked the rugs vacuumed religiously.

Another text came in, and Jane checked it. The job applicant had responded, agreeing to the interview time. Jane put the vacuum away, then went into the kitchen and started to methodically clean.

By the time she was finished with the Daleys another hour had passed, which meant that Cameron should have definitely been out of the appointment, even if the office was running behind.

She climbed into her car and tried not to think about what this delay could mean. Maybe the doctor was late, or maybe Cameron was talking to Crystal about future arrangements. Or maybe . . . She blinked against the stinging in her eyes.

Once she reached her next client, an older woman who lived in a condo by herself, Jane resolved to not think about Cameron and Crystal for the next hour. She cleaned Mrs. Burnett's house with vigor, getting corners and areas that had likely not been cleaned since the place was built.

She was a sweaty mess when she finished, but it had

helped take her mind off things. Still, Cameron hadn't called. Maybe he'd forgotten? Got caught up with business, or something? But they'd texted each other just that morning, and Cameron had said he'd call Jane after the appointment.

Jane heaved a sigh and loaded her cleaning kit into the trunk of her car. Then she headed home to take a shower. She was grateful to find her dad on the phone with someone when she came into the house. She was too keyed up to have any sort of normal conversation with her dad; he'd know that something was off.

She showered and dressed. Cameron still hadn't called. Now she was annoyed. What was he doing? Why wasn't he calling her? She couldn't stand not knowing . . . even if the news was bad. She told her dad she was going to run some errands. Then she started her car and headed toward Cameron's.

She hoped he was home so that she could find out what was going on. But then again, if he was home, why hadn't he called her?

When she pulled up to his cabin, there were no lights on. So, maybe he wasn't home. Was he still with Crystal?

Jane sat in the car for a moment, then gathered up her courage and got out. She knocked on the front door. There was no sound or movement. The sound of an approaching car drew her attention, and she turned to see a car coming up the lane to the cabin. It took only seconds to figure out that it was Cameron.

She wondered if he was alone, or maybe he and Crystal were in some deep conversation about their child.

Jane felt like a fool showing up like this. She couldn't move as she watched the car approach. By now, he would have seen her car parked to the side of the driveway. The garage door started to open, and Cameron pulled into the garage.

Jane decided to wait on the porch until he went inside and shut the garage. Then she'd make her getaway. Suddenly she didn't want to confront him. Her tears were already starting, and she just needed to be by herself.

"Jane?" Cameron said, coming through the front of the garage.

Too late. She froze as he saw her on the porch. She gazed at him, trying to read his expression, trying to understand what had been going on.

"Hi," she said at last. "I was just checking on you since you never called."

Cameron looked away, rubbing the back of his neck. "Yeah. It's been a hell of a day."

Jane felt like she was shrinking. She bit her lip, wondering how she could gracefully move past Cameron and leave.

His eyes were back on her. "I have sort of a long story to tell you."

Dread pooled in her stomach, and she felt like she was going to be sick.

"Do you want to come in?" he asked.

No, she wanted to say. "Okay."

Cameron continued up the steps and walked past her. He didn't try to touch her or kiss her. He merely used his key to unlock the front door.

The interior was dim, with the western light of the sky nearly gone. He walked into the kitchen, and Jane followed, feeling like a lonely dog following its master.

"Do you want something to drink?" he asked.

"No," Jane croaked out. She wrapped her arms about her torso, unsure if she should stand or sit.

Cameron opened a water bottle and guzzled down the whole thing. Then he crunched it and tossed it into the trash.

He turned and braced his hands on the counter across from where Jane stood.

His head dropped forward, and Jane wanted to leave—she didn't want to hear Cameron say the words . . .

"She's not pregnant," Cameron said in a quiet tone.

A jolt shot through Jane. "W-what?"

Cameron lifted his head, and in the dimness of the kitchen, she could see the tears in his eyes. What did this mean? Crystal had lied? She'd miscarried? Was Cameron heartbroken over it?

"She's what my mother said she was," Cameron said, his voice stronger now. "She was trying to get back together with me. When I got to the doctor's office, Crystal didn't show. She texted me about a half hour after the appointment time and said she wasn't feeling well, and she'd reschedule later. So I talked to the receptionist about rescheduling, and I was told there was never an appointment in the first place."

Jane stared at Cameron. His tone was full of bitterness, and that somehow comforted Jane. But the pain in his gaze was heart wrenching.

"I went back to my car and called Crystal," he continued. "She didn't answer at first. I texted her, then waited and called her again. Finally, she answered, and she did sound sick . . . or so I thought. She told me the receptionist had been mistaken."

Jane moved to one of the barstools and slipped into it. Cameron remained standing.

"I had an awful feeling that wouldn't go away," he said. "Just like I did when those men delivering furniture arrived here. I called my mom and told her what happened. She told me to go get a pregnancy test and make Crystal take it while I was at her house."

Jane's eyes widened. "Did you?"

He nodded, rubbing at his neck again. "I think I sat outside of the pharmacy for an hour before I went inside."

Jane would have helped him, had he called her. She waited for him to continue.

"I knew it was kind of a crazy move, but I went for it." He looked down at the counter and didn't speak for a long time.

"You don't have to tell me everything," Jane finally said.

He lifted his head and wiped at his eyes. "She was home, and at first she tried to kick me out. I threatened to hire a lawyer to get an order that would force her to take the test."

"A lawyer can do that?" she asked.

Cameron shrugged. "I don't know. I was pretty desperate, so I bluffed my way through. She took the box from me and disappeared down the hall. I stayed by the door in case she became hysterical for whatever reason."

When he faded off again, Jane rose from her stool and walked around the counter. She placed a hand on his back. He didn't seem to mind, so Jane took that as a good sign.

"She came out about fifteen minutes later, crying." He took a deep breath. "She hadn't even opened the pregnancy test. Instead, she threw it at me and then started throwing other stuff."

Jane drew away from him, looking more closely at him. "Were you hurt?"

"I'm pretty good at ducking," he said in a dry voice. "But I refused to leave until she told me the truth. Finally, she screamed, 'I'm not pregnant, now are you happy?'"

"I don't even know what to say," Jane said.

"I've got to be the most gullible man in the world." His tone had sharpened with anger now.

"I'm sure you're not the first man to be lied to that way," Jane said. "How are you to know, unless you do see the test or an ultrasound?"

"Yeah, I know, I just feel like . . . like she could have continued to string me along, and when would I have found out?" Cameron straightened. "Plus, I let this mess affect my relationship with you."

When he reached for her, Jane had no problem melting into his arms. "It's not your fault, Cameron. You're a good man, and sometimes good men are taken advantage of."

"You sound like my mom."

Jane drew away enough to look up at him. "Is that a good thing?"

The distress in his eyes had lessened, and he bent closer to her. "It's a good thing. I'm really sorry for all of this."

"Don't apologize for anything," Jane said. "I'm just glad you're finally free of Crystal."

He nodded. "Me too. Although I sort of feel like I lost a kid."

"Of course you do," she said, moving her hands up his chest, then settling them on his shoulders. "You'd already accepted the pregnancy in your mind and were making plans for the future."

Cameron pulled her into a tight hug and buried his face against her neck. "Do you know you always smell good?"

Jane chuckled. "So do you." And he did. She was glad she'd come to his cabin too. Cameron was much better in person than Cameron any other way.

Twenty-one

"How soon is too soon?" Cameron asked his friend, Jeff Finch, while they had a late lunch together at the Main Street Café.

"To ask a woman to marry you?" Jeff said, a lopsided smile on his face.

Cameron glared at his friend, who thought he was some big real estate hot shot now and could give him a hard time. "No. How soon is too soon to know if what you have with a woman is the real thing? Something that will last forever?"

"Ah," Jeff said. "As if I'm some sort of love expert. Why don't you Google it?"

"Ha. Ha. Very funny." Cameron sipped from his soda. "I mean, I've only been seeing Jane for a few weeks. But it's as if my whole world has shifted."

"Maybe you're on the rebound from Crystal," Jeff said.

"Yeah, I've considered that too," Cameron admitted. "But my parents have told me she's different from any of my former girlfriends, and that I'm different too. I feel that difference."

Jeff took another bite of the BLT he'd ordered. "Then you tell me, man. What's different about how you feel about Jane versus how you felt about Crystal—whom you almost married?"

It was a valid question, and Cameron leaned back in his chair, thinking about it. Their personalities and backgrounds were different, of course. Their moral compasses were complete opposites. With Crystal, Cameron felt like she was driving everything, practically forcing them through the steps toward engagement and marriage. Now that he was away from it, Cameron could see how stifled he'd been and how controlling Crystal had been too.

With Jane, he felt like he couldn't get enough time with her. He missed her almost as soon as he left her, and she was the first thing he thought about when he woke up in the morning.

"I care more about her well-being than my own," Cameron finally told Jeff. "I know it sounds cliché, but when we're apart, I feel like something is missing. Like my heart." He expected Jeff to laugh, but when he didn't, Cameron added, "I'm whipped, huh?"

"Um, yep," Jeff said. "But I'm happy for you. I can see the difference in you too. You're more happy, more relaxed, more focused." Jeff grabbed his own soda and took a long swallow. "So I think you're pretty much good to go."

"Good to go for what?" Cameron said.

"To make the big confession," Jeff said with a grin, then leaned forward. "Tell her how you feel. Declare your love!" He winked.

Cameron chuckled, then looked down at his half-eaten sandwich, knowing there was no way he could finish it off.

Not with his stomach tied in knots. "I want to tell her—but I've been holding back for some reason. She's putting down a deposit on an apartment today and signing a one-year lease. I want to tell her not to do it, because I want her future to be with me, but am I just feeling this push because she's about to sign a lease?"

"Maybe. Or maybe it has to do with your relationship with Crystal," Jeff said, straightening in his chair. "I'm no psychologist, but if you told Crystal you loved her, and she ended up being a major witch, then how do you go from that experience to loving a different woman? How can you trust your emotions?"

"Now I know why you're the best realtor in Pine Valley," Cameron said. "You get people."

"So, I'm right?"

Cameron nodded. "You're right. And I've put this off for far too long. I want Jane to know . . . the truth about how I feel. I want her to know that she belongs with me."

"You should tell her sooner than later," Jeff said. "And not because she's signing a lease today. Jane's a beautiful woman. Bringing her to that benefit caught a lot of men's attention."

Disbelief shot through Cameron. "You wouldn't dare—"

"Not me," Jeff said, raising his hands in innocence. "But I can't speak for others."

Cameron exhaled. "You're a jerk."

Jeff laughed. "Hey, don't forget I bought lunch. Maybe next time it should be on you."

Cameron shook his head. "All right, I'm going to do this. Today. Somehow I'm going to do it before she meets with the leasing company."

"Good for you," Jeff said. "I really mean it."

Cameron stood and picked up his plate of half-eaten food. "Thanks, man."

Jeff just smiled and nodded. "Let me know what she says, or doesn't say . . ."

"Ha. Ha." Cameron carried his plate to the trash. Then with a final acknowledgment to Jeff, he left the café.

He climbed into his car. He had two conference calls soon, and then he hoped to catch Jane before she went to the leasing office. He didn't know if telling her how he truly felt about her would change things, but he didn't want to think of her locked into a one-year contract. What if . . . what if they decided to get married? He didn't want to wait a year.

And yes, he knew contracts could be sold or paid out, but this was giving him incentive to cross that line from dating to exclusivity. Not that he thought Jane would date anyone else, especially with the way she kissed him. But he was being selfish, and he wanted her all to himself. Forever.

Cameron started his car and drove back to his cabin. Was he really wanting to marry Jane? It might sound crazy, but he knew he did. He didn't want to scare her off, though. So he'd take it slower than he wanted to.

When he reached the cabin, he went inside and opened his laptop to take notes during the conference calls. Each of the calls lasted about an hour. Then he noticed he had a reply to a series of emails he'd sent the week before to an art college that was about an hour's drive away. He'd started researching it without telling Jane.

It turned out that the college was expensive, but students who didn't get accepted on scholarship could continue applying each semester. There were also evening and weekend classes, so it could fit in with Jane's work schedule.

Cameron opened the email and read through the acceptance letter. They'd received the watercolor Cameron had mailed them—the watercolor Jane had done of the women in the assisted living center. He'd talked Jane into giving it to him to put in his cabin, and she'd reluctantly agreed. Cameron opened the attached PDF and followed the instructions for registering for part-time credits and paying tuition.

He didn't know if Jane would accept the opportunity, and he knew he could request a tuition refund, minus the application fee, but if everything was done, then maybe Jane would be more willing to try it. He sent the acceptance letter and class schedule to the printer, then stuck it all in a large envelope.

It was after 5:00, so he sent Jane a text, knowing she should be almost finished for the day: *Do you want to meet for dinner when you're finished with work?*

She replied a few minutes later: *I can later. The leasing office closes at 6:00, so I have to go there first.*

Can you go tomorrow? he wrote back.

They're only holding the place for me until closing today.

Cameron exhaled. He had to reach her before she signed those papers. He powered down the laptop, then grabbed the oversized envelope. He headed out the door again to hopefully intercept Jane before she signed any leasing papers.

There was no sign of her car when he pulled into the leasing office parking lot. So he sat and waited, answering various texts and emails on his phone. His pulse drummed as he waited, and he was about to call her when he saw her car approaching.

Cameron climbed out of his car just as Jane climbed out of hers. She did a double take when she saw him. She was still wearing her cleaning uniform.

Her smile gave him another bit of courage, and Cameron crossed the parking lot.

"I didn't know you were coming," Jane said. "You must be really hungry."

"Mostly just impatient," he said, setting the envelope he carried on top of her car. Then he grasped her hand and tugged her toward him.

She raised her eyebrows but came easily in his arms. "What's up with you?"

He stared into her green eyes. Then his gaze dipped to her mouth. "I missed you."

Jane ran her fingers along his neck, then her thumb against his jaw. "You're funny, you know that. I mean, we saw each other last night."

Cameron placed a light kiss on her lips. "That was last night."

"Do you want to come inside with me?" she asked, starting to draw away from his hold.

"No," he said.

"Okay, I'll probably be about twenty minutes. Then we can get something to eat."

"Jane," he said, stopping her from pulling out of his arms. "I need to talk to you."

Jane's eyes immediately filled with concern.

"It's not anything bad," he said. "At least, I hope not."

When her brows pulled together, he knew he was making things worse.

"Just tell me, Cameron. All of this preamble is killing me."

"Right." He released her and grabbed the envelope from on top of the car. "I got you a small gift, but before you open it, I need to tell you something." He handed over the plain envelope.

"Okay," Jane said, looking down at the envelope, then back at him.

A car pulled into the parking lot, and Cameron glanced over. He waited until the man who climbed out of the car entered the leasing office. Cameron could feel Jane's gaze on him.

"Look," he started, "I know when we met I was sort of going through a crazy time. And I probably wasn't really myself. In fact, I don't think I was myself the entire relationship with Crystal. And then . . . things ended with us. And I started to get to know you."

Jane nodded, her gaze curious. But she was gripping the envelope less tightly.

"Of course I noticed you—I mean, who wouldn't?" he said. "You're beautiful, but most importantly, you listened to me, you helped me when you didn't even know me. Which only showed me how huge your heart is."

Jane blinked a couple of times, and her cheeks took on a faint pink tinge.

"So . . . I wanted to give you something that I'm hoping you'll want," he said. "You've told me more than once that we come from different backgrounds and walks of life, but I only think that makes us stronger. Your strengths help me, and hopefully, my strengths can help you."

Jane smiled. "Can I open it now?"

"Soon," he said, grasping her hand. He linked their fingers, and the physical connection helped him continue. "I was engaged to Crystal, and even though I had planned on marrying her, I didn't know what love was. I didn't understand the difference between the excitement of being caught up in planning a future together, and the definition of love when two people put each other's needs before their own."

"Cameron . . ." Jane's voice trailed off when he placed a finger to her lips.

"I can't wait another day without telling you that I've fallen in love with you, Jane," he said.

Her eyes widened, and her smile fell from her face.

It wasn't the reaction Cameron had hoped for. "I think I've loved you since our first dance at the hospital benefit, but I couldn't fathom feeling that type of emotion after what I'd been through."

Jane looked down at their linked hands.

"I know this might be too soon to say these things, and I've been trying not to move things forward too fast, but it's killing me," he said. She still wasn't looking at him. "I'll understand if I've freaked you out and you want to tell me to go take a hike."

Jane lifted her face, and she had tears in her eyes. She blinked them back, but the sight still tugged at his heart.

Cameron had spoken too soon. He should have given their relationship more time.

But instead of telling him that he couldn't possibly feel this way, she placed her other hand on his cheek. "I don't want you to disappear, Cameron. I'm okay with what you're telling me, because I love you too."

He stared at her for a moment. Then he grabbed her and spun her around.

Jane clung to his shoulders and laughed. "Put me down."

So he did, but not before kissing her thoroughly.

"Now can I open the envelope?" she asked.

He took a deep breath. "Yes, please."

She grinned at him, then opened the top of the envelope. She pulled out the stapled papers inside. "What is this?"

He didn't answer, just let her read through the acceptance letter.

"What did you do?" she asked, looking up at him.

"Turn the page," he said, hoping that this had been a good move.

She turned the page and gasped. "You paid the tuition? And . . ." She flipped to the third page. "I'm registered?"

"You can change the classes if you want, but the guidance counselor said these are core classes that are required for the more advanced courses."

She was still staring at the list of classes. "How . . . how did they accept me? It's been years since I've done any serious art."

Cameron shoved his hands in his pockets. Here came the hard part. "I sent them your watercolor."

She looked up at him, her green eyes wide. "This is . . . This is . . ." She took a deep breath. "What about my job?"

"This is only a part-time schedule. There's one class on Saturdays, and the other two are evening classes," Cameron explained. "A lot of people go to college when they're still working a full-time job. But maybe you wouldn't have to work full-time since the tuition is already paid for."

Jane opened her mouth, then shut it. Finally, she said, "This is not a scholarship. You paid the tuition?"

"I did," he said, expecting her rejection. "I can get my money back if you don't want to do this. But I don't want my money back." He raised his hand to tuck a stray strand of her hair behind her ear. "You're an amazing artist and a great business woman, Jane. You can do anything. I just want to help you get there."

Jane exhaled, then waved the papers in front of her as she blinked her eyes. "Cameron, I just don't know. I mean, this is wonderful, generous. It would take me forever to pay you back."

"I don't want you to pay me back," Cameron said. "And I'm hoping that you won't sign that lease either."

Her eyes connected with his. "What? Why not?"

"Because a year would be way too long to wait to marry you."

Jane went absolutely still. "What did you say?" she whispered.

"I said, I love you," he said. "And don't sign the lease, because I'm going to ask you to marry me soon—when I know you'll say *yes*. It might be too soon now, but a year will be way too long."

Jane brought a hand to her mouth, and she seemed to be trying to catch her breath. Then she turned away.

"Jane?" Cameron asked after a moment.

Slowly she turned around. She wiped the tears from her eyes, then threw her arms around his neck.

Twenty-two

Jane applied her final touches of makeup. Tonight was game night with her dad at the assisted living center. It had been Bea's birthday earlier this week, so Jane had made cupcakes, and she was wearing a pink blouse in honor of Bea. Jane had also found some silver, heeled sandals, since silver was Bea's second favorite color.

The woman would get a kick out of it. Jane had bought a beginner's oil painting kit as a birthday present for Bea. Even though the woman's hands weren't steady, she had talent in painting. Jane had also bought five small canvas boxes that contained pre-printed images that Bea could practice oil painting on.

"Are you ready, Jane?" her dad's gravelly voice echoed from the kitchen.

"Coming!" she called out as she put on her earrings. She was wearing her hair down, and she applied a final spritz of her favorite apple blossom scent, which of course made her think of Cameron. He always said she smelled good.

Cameron had been hinting at proposing all week, until Jane was about to ask him herself. Three weeks had passed since that day in the leasing center parking lot. Jane had been overwhelmed, and thrilled, and astounded . . . And she could only hope that she was seeing their relationship for what it really was, that she wasn't just being swept off her feet.

Jane hadn't signed the lease. Perhaps she was being too hopeful. But if things fell apart she could find another place. She knew she should have more faith, but it was difficult when her parents had divorced and her mother had been a serial dater. Yet, when Jane was around Cameron, she saw the sincerity in his brown eyes and heard the truth in his words. He loved her, and it was heady to think about.

Cameron had said nothing about a ring, but with all the hints he'd been dropping, and considering that they had plans next weekend to go to another charity gala hosted by his mom, Jane wondered if he'd ask the big question there.

She grabbed her purse from the bed before her dad took it upon himself to shuffle down to her room. Then she picked up the present she'd carefully wrapped in pink-and-white polka-dotted paper—another thing Bea would appreciate.

"You're looking spruced up," she said as soon as she saw her dad.

He wore a polo shirt and khakis with his best leather belt. "It's Bea's birthday."

"Yes, it is," Jane said, raising her brows.

"I like the pink," her dad said, waving a hand at her ensemble.

Compliments were rare from her dad. "Oh, thanks. Bea's favorite color."

Her dad chuckled. "She makes no secret of that."

Jane smiled. It seemed her dad was in a very good mood tonight. "Ready?" She grabbed the container of cupcakes.

As they headed out of the house, Jane breathed in the crisp air. Fall was just around the corner, and the leaves had started to change in the neighborhood. The ski resort was already a riot of orange, red, and yellow. She probably should grab her dad a jacket, but he might turn grumpy again if she delayed any longer. Besides, she could just warm up the car for a few minutes before they drove home tonight.

She set the cupcakes on the back seat. "Remember—"

"I know," her dad said. "Only one cupcake." His tone was light and obedient.

Again, Jane was surprised.

On their way over, Jane knew she'd miss Cameron tonight. He'd been coming every Saturday to game night, but he was in San Francisco over the weekend for some board meetings. They'd had a lot of talks about the art college, and Jane was starting in January, at which point she hoped to turn more work hours over to her part-time employee. It was a new experience having an employee, and Cameron had been great with advice on that.

She sighed as she pulled into the parking lot of the center. Tonight wouldn't be the same without Cameron here, but she was determined to make it a fabulous evening with Bea.

Jane parked and climbed out of the car. She helped her dad up and got him situated with his cane, then grabbed the cupcakes.

Once inside, Jane took the cupcakes to the main kitchen so she could keep them a surprise. The center had likely made her a cake earlier in the week when it was her actual birthday. As she entered the gathering room with her dad, Pete waved them over to the card table right away. Jane crossed to the table with her dad, and Pete said, "Do you have one of those cell phone things with you that plays music?"

"I do," Jane said, reaching for it in her pocket.

"Not now." Pete waved her off. "I want this to be a surprise. We're going to have a dance, and I'm going to ask Bea to dance with me."

"Oh?" Jane said with a grin. "When?"

"In about an hour," Pete said.

"Okay, great," Jane said. "I brought some cupcakes. We'll sing 'Happy Birthday,' then I'll break out my music." She looked about the room. "Do you think I could hook it up to the speakers so everyone can hear it?"

Pete shrugged. "You'll have to ask the staff."

Jane did and found that one of the staff members had a bluetooth speaker.

Jane made her way over to the art table. Bea was already beaming because she obviously knew that the present Jane carried was for her. Bea wore a bright pink blouse with a paisley print that Jane suspected was a couple of decades old. The woman's yellow hair was topped by her usual sparkly silver headband.

"Well, look at you," Bea said. "We almost match."

"It was your birthday a few days ago, so I decided to dress in your favorite colors."

Bea laughed, and when Jane set her present before Bea, she said, "What's this?"

"Happy birthday," Jane said.

Bea giggled as she tore at the wrapping paper, and then she *oo*'d when she saw the oil painting kit. "Can you show me how to use it?"

"Of course," Jane said.

"Tonight?" Bea asked.

"Sure, why not?"

The other ladies exclaimed over the kit and said they wanted to try too.

Jane opened the kit and set to work. Soon, they were all

dabbing brushes into one of the oil colors, and painting on the canvas boxes Jane had passed out. She'd bring more next week. She was glad the beginner's kit had low-scent paints in it.

When the women had made good progress on their canvases, Jane went to get the cupcakes from the kitchen. She handed over her phone to the staff member to pull up the "Happy Birthday" song. When the music started, Jane came back into the room with the cupcakes.

Bea clapped her hands in delight, and everyone started singing. After the song and cupcakes, Pete came over to the art table.

He cleared his throat and said in his scratchy voice, "Bea, I'd like to ask you to dance a birthday dance with me."

Bea stared at him. "There's no music, Pete."

Pete turned to the staff member who was handling the music and gave the signal. He started the playlist on Jane's phone, and music filled the room.

Bea grinned and put her hand into Pete's. She rose.

Jane tugged back an empty table to give them more room. She looked over at her dad to see him smiling. A few others stood and started to dance—in modified versions of how they might have danced if they were younger. The women at the art table danced together, and those who weren't so steady on their feet tapped the table with fingers, or the floor with toes.

Jane laughed. Bea was smiling wide, and Pete's face was flushed. The next song started, and Jane found herself swaying to the music. It was hard to just stand and watch. The music was contagious, and everyone in the room was enjoying it. Jane mostly enjoyed watching Bea and Pete. How had she never seen that Pete obviously had a crush on the woman?

Song after song played, and the residents were fully enjoying the dancing. The staff even joined in.

When Jane felt someone's arms slide around her from behind, she yelped.

"Hey," Cameron said into her ear.

She turned in his arms. "What are you doing here?"

His brown eyes were merry as he scanned her face. "I heard about this rocking party and thought I'd come over."

"But, I thought you were in San Francisco until next week," she said, looping her arms about his neck. She inhaled his spicy scent that was unique to Cameron.

"I missed you," he said.

"Yeah, but what about work?" she asked.

"I'll head back tomorrow," he said and pulled her closer.

"Everyone's watching us," Jane said, wondering if he was going to kiss her right there in the middle of everyone.

"Yeah, I know." Cameron leaned down and kissed her.

The kiss was brief, too brief. But that was probably good, because, well, her dad was just a few feet away from them. And even though her dad wholeheartedly approved of Cameron, Jane wasn't into PDA so much.

"Did your meetings get canceled or something?" she asked.

"I canceled them," he said with a shrug. "I had something really important to do."

Jane raised her brows.

"This morning on my way to the first meeting, I passed by a jewelry store," he said. "I happened to glance at the windows, and I had to stop."

Jane blinked. "Why?"

One side of his mouth lifted into a smile. "I saw the perfect ring."

Jane couldn't speak. Was he talking about an *engagement* ring?

He released her, and at this action, Jane's pulse rate

doubled. Yep, he was reaching into his pocket, and yep, he was pulling out a small velvet box.

"Cameron," she breathed.

"It's the most beautiful ring I've ever seen, and it reminded me of you," he continued.

Jane's eyes pricked with tears. Why did he want to show her the ring at this assisted living place? And why would he cancel his meetings to drive back and show her?

"Jane, you know I love you," he said.

Jane could only nod. She was well aware everyone around them could see and hear everything that was going on. She almost expected her dad to interrupt, but no word came from him.

Then Cameron knelt down, and Jane couldn't breathe.

"Marry me, Jane," he said. "I know without a doubt that we belong together." He broke eye contact to open the ring box.

Jane couldn't see any details of the diamond ring because her vision was blurry.

"If you don't like it, we can find something else," he said, looking up again. "But I couldn't wait another minute to ask you to be my wife."

Jane covered her mouth. Her heart was beating so hard, she wondered if it would burst out of her chest. "I—I didn't expect . . ."

"Say yes," someone called out, and Jane was almost positive it was her dad. But she couldn't take her eyes from Cameron's beseeching expression. She loved this man, more than she ever thought she could love someone.

Cameron didn't move, and it was like everyone in the room was waiting with him.

"Yes," she whispered.

Cameron grinned and was on his feet in a second, pulling

her into his arms. As he kissed her fiercely, the people around them cheered.

Jane kissed him back, closing her eyes and wrapping her arms around him.

More cheering, and Jane broke away, laughing.

"Dance with me?" Cameron asked.

"Of course, but first, let me see that ring."

Cameron pulled the ring out of the velvet box.

The ring was beautiful. The solitaire sat in a diamond-studded silver band. Cameron slid it on her ring finger, and Jane felt warm chills all the way down her spine. The music shifted to a slower song with perfect timing.

"You surprised me," Jane said as Cameron pulled her into his arms and started to slowly sway to the music.

"I hope it was a good surprise," he whispered against her ear.

"It was the best surprise," she whispered back. She looked past Cameron to see her dad sitting at his game table with a big smile on his face.

Not too far away, Pete and Bea were still dancing. Pete winked at her as their gazes connected.

Jane smiled and nestled closer to Cameron, who was only too happy to oblige.

"What do you think about a Christmas wedding?" Cameron asked.

Jane looked at him and quirked an eyebrow. "I think our moms would have a heart attack."

Cameron chuckled. "Maybe we should just elope then."

Jane ran one of her hands over his shoulder. "My mom would definitely kill me. I think she already has my wedding dress picked out."

"Okay, okay," Cameron said. "I'll stop making suggestions, but I also don't want to wait too long."

"Yeah, I figured that out," Jane said with a laugh. "Do you always get what you want?"

He shrugged. "Not always, but all I need is you. Nothing else matters."

"Hmmm," Jane said. "Well, you have me, Mr. Vance."

When Cameron kissed her for the third time on the makeshift dance floor, Jane let herself melt into his arms. What did it matter that they had an audience? Everyone here would be invited to the wedding, and they'd be seeing plenty more of Jane and Cameron kissing.

About Heather B. Moore

Heather B. Moore is a four-time *USA Today* bestselling author. She writes historical thrillers under the pen name H.B. Moore; her latest thrillers include *The Killing Curse* and *Poetic Justice*. Under the name Heather B. Moore, she writes romance and women's fiction. Her newest releases include the historical romance *Love is Come*. She's also one of the coauthors of the *USA Today* bestselling series: A Timeless Romance Anthology. Heather writes speculative fiction under the pen name Jane Redd; releases include the Solstice series and *Mistress Grim*. Heather is represented by Dystel, Goderich & Bourret.

For book updates, sign up for Heather's email list:
hbmoore.com/contact
Website: HBMoore.com
Facebook: Fans of H. B. Moore
Blog: MyWritersLair.blogspot.com
Instagram: @authorhbmoore
Twitter: @HeatherBMoore

MORE PINE VALLEY SERIES:

Made in the USA
San Bernardino, CA
09 February 2019